# Craig Brackenridge

Stormscreen Productions

First Published in 2009 by
STORMSCREEN PRODUCTIONS
Retford,
Notts DN22 0JL

Email: brackotrashcan@hotmail.co.uk
Website: www.myspace.com/stormscreenproductions

This work is Copyright Craig Brackenridge, 2009

ISBN: 978-0-9546249-2-7

All rights reserved. No part of this book may be reproduced or transmitted in any form or by any means, electronic or mechanical, including photocopying, recording or any information storage and retrieval system, without permission in writing from the publisher.

This book is sold subject to the condition that it shall not, by way of trade or otherwise, be lent, resold, hired out or otherwise circulated without the publisher's prior consent in any form of binding or cover other than that in which it was published and without a similar condition being imposed on the subsequent purchaser.

The moral right of the author has been asserted.

British Library Cataloguing-in-Publication Data
A catalogue for this book is available from the British Library

Cover Star: Russ Surfer (www.punkabilly.co.uk)

Designed and printed by www.burgessdesignandprint.com
Retford, Tel: 01777 860579

# Contents

| | | |
|---|---|---|
| Foreword. | | Page 5 |
| Chapter 1: | New Town Knuckle Shuffle | Page 7 |
| Chapter 2: | The Psychobilly Disease | Page 13 |
| Chapter 3: | Oi Thatcher! Up Yours! | Page 21 |
| Chapter 4: | Klub Foot Stompin' - Wham! Bam! Thank-you Pam! | Page 26 |
| Chapter 5: | Boots, Bottles and Blades | Page 44 |
| Chapter 6: | Sex Beat Crazy | Page 54 |
| Chapter 7: | Squeeze Play | Page 64 |
| Chapter 8: | The Spirit of 69 | Page 74 |
| Chapter 9: | Seaside Special | Page 87 |
| Chapter 10: | Self-destruction Blues | Page 99 |
| Chapter 11: | Here We Are Nowhere | Page 106 |
| Chapter 12: | Never Lose It | Page 115 |

# Acknowledgements

Dedicated to I, P & F once again.

Big thanks once again to Russ Ward and Jo Jackson for their continued support.

Extra big thanks to all the following who showed enough faith in the book to cough up in advance. Cheers! Hope thee enjoy it:

Kev Starie (1st Sale), Pete Davis, Gary Wheeler,
Matt Galloway, Mainy, Laura Smith, Popo from France,
Linda Devine, Catford Bob, Dave Scrivener,
Pete Flory (Ciderman), Phil Benson, Darren Groves,
Nathan Barfboy, Mark Jakins, Paul Spowart,
Dixie / Andy G, Ian Smith, Madman - Psychobilly Online,
Koefte, Andrew Phillips, Rothwell Jase, Sam Woods,
Ted Marshall, Nigel Poole - Good Wreckin' Tonight,
Mike & Julia McMahon, Fatbloke, Stevie Hannah,
DJ Chris Setzer, Baz from Huddersfield, Andy Gailey,
Jo Shalton, Malc Pike, Slinger, Big Keith
and The Black Puma.

# Foreword

When my Mum and Dad moved to Stevenage in the 1960's it was something of a 'Brave New World' for young families who were looking to make a break from the overcrowded shit-hole that the capital was becoming. London may have been swinging for middle-class groovers and shiftless hippies squatting in mansions but for working-class punters like my Dad on £8 a week it meant three to a room, a kitchen so small that your arse stuck out the back door when you bent down to open the oven, and a trip to a freezing outhouse at the bottom of the garden every time you needed a shit.

Stevenage was a way out for my parents. A shiny New Town with bright, modernist housing. Big windows, split levels, patios and even a driveway for a car (which we did not have). New schools, less traffic, safe walkways for pedestrians and a whole lot of other bullshit was served up to them in glossy brochures by idealistic town planners and development corporations who would eventually skip town like gypsies in the night as soon as their New Town ideals started to tarnish. My Mum and Dad made the move to Stevenage with the best intentions, to make a new start for the Powell family and to give my sister and I a better chance in life. Somewhere green for us to play, a new school and better opportunities. They did not know that the whole thing would turn to shit when the developers moved their idealistic dreams onto their next project and occasionally dozy housing officers would flood the town with the worst human flotsam that London estates could not wait to get rid of. How could my folks possibly know that in the rush to build this gleaming metropolis, builders on 'piece work' were knocking together housing like fucking Meccano kits with half the bits left in the box.

Once, late at night on BBC2, I saw a film that

was made in Stevenage in the late 1960's. It starred that bloke from 'Mind Your Language' and it was full of fresh looking dolly birds and young geezers having a good time. Everything looked fresh & new, the shops and houses were sparkling clean and people were shagging at parties and zipping about in sports cars, laughing and generally having a good fucking time.

Its not like that in 1986. Coming home from the chippy near the town square tonight I had to dodge a mob of blonde-streaked trendies who were hanging around the bus station looking for trouble. Then I brushed passed some begging junkies in a piss-soaked underpass and finally reached my house, where I settled down in my room where the walls are so thin I can hear my Dad scratching his arse in the room next door and the windows are as damp as a strumpet's fanny. Don't get me wrong, I am not some whining, socially deprived youth or a victim of some pot-smoking social engineers. I have a great life. I love Stevenage. My mum and dad got the New Town dream but I got something a lot more worthwhile. I got Psychobilly.

# Chapter 1
# New Town Knuckle Shuffle

I was thundering down the concrete walkway as fast as I could. My legs were burning but sheer fear and adrenalin drove me on. This was far faster than I had ever run on the school playing fields, as our half-bent P.E. teacher Mr Blakey shouted encouragement and praised our half-hearted sprinting techniques while counting down the minutes until he could 'supervise' us coming out of the showers. Its funny how being chased by five pissed-up posers, tanked up on supermarket-strength lager and desperate to stamp on your head with their slip-on shoes, can increase your athletic prowess.

Difference is not something that is celebrated much in Stevenage. It may be something which is embraced around the table at dinner parties in the posh houses up in Bandley Hill but in the near deserted concrete canyons of the town centre late on a Tuesday night it is strictly them and us. "They" are five unidentifiable members of the local pond life and part of the town's huge population of half-wits who rely on football players, Top Of The Pops and the local Burton's for their identity. "I" am one of Stevenage's growing Psychobilly clan, a small but perfectly formed gang of ex-Punks, Skinheads and Rockabillies who think ourselves a step above the rest of the local alternative types, as we cast a mocking glare at the disparate bands of Goths and Heavy Metal freaks who are spread across town. There are some complex rivalries and allegiances across the youth tribes of Stevenage but tonight it is simply oil and water. I have a seven-inch dyed blonde quiff, shaved to a number one at the back and sides, and clad in the standard uniform: Doc Marten boots, tight bleached denims and a Meteors' T-shirt. The half-wits are a furious bundle of streaked hair, pastel shirts and bum-fluff moustaches.

I was caught walking across the town square alone. Captured in their sights from where they sat boozing. Giving me a kicking must have seemed far more exciting than talking shit all night and carving their names on a bench. The abuse and name-calling was relatively brief as they had obviously made their minds up that beating me senseless would alleviate the boredom. 'Stand and fight, never bottle it' might be what they say on the terraces but fuck that when it is five on one and I am stone cold sober. I had it off on my toes.

The longer that I ran made the spectre of some pretty brutal physical contact ever more likely. As I pelted down Market Place past the tightly shuttered shops I had one of those blinding flashes of insight that occasionally accompanies sheer panic. I headed straight for the underpass that led to the church. A long, dark tunnel that I knew could either offer me salvation or the opportunity for a prolonged kicking away from any prying eyes or local coppers. I knew that my enforced session of long-distance running was coming to an end anyway as adrenalin was rapidly being replaced with exhaustion and the effect of too many roll-ups in my teenage years was leading to a leaden feeling in my legs.

The gentle reek of urine greeted me as I entered the underpass and I could almost feel the booze-soaked breath of my pursuers on my neck. I noticed two figures at the end of the tunnel and as I moved towards the light I could pick out two unmistakeable flat-tops. White T-shirts, denims, boots… my heart lifted and I felt a renewed rush of excitement.

'Knocker! Vince! Casuals!' I shouted and saw that my plight dawned on them immediately as they saw the hunting party behind me.

I heard one of them shout, 'It's Harry,' and they

dropped their cans of Breaker and moved towards me unflinchingly to offer support.

I stopped running and turned quickly then there was a mighty dull thud as eight bodies collided in the semi-darkness twelve feet below the town's busy ring road. Ever the traditionalist, Knocker used his tried and tested technique of wrapping his beefy hands around the neck of the largest member of the opposition then head butting them in the face. It may be rather crude but yet again it proved invaluable as it took their biggest man out of the picture immediately as he dropped to the ground nursing his broken nose with blood dripping through his fingers. Vince and I had less finesse than our burly amigo and instead settled for blindly lashing out with fists and boots at anything in a pair of Farah slacks. By the time Knocker had floored another of my tormentors with his grip and smash technique they seemed to lose their enthusiasm a bit and the three that could still run did a bunk.

We kicked the other two around for a bit but eventually we were happy to move back to Vince and Knocker's carrier bag full of booze. Both casuals eventually struggled to their feet and moved back the way they came. As I cracked open a can I recognised that one of them had been in my woodwork class a few years back when I was still at Collenswood Secondary. He was alright back then but things had changed now. Psychobilly had hit my life like a hurricane and I was a different person than the little Herbert I had been at school. I looked down and noticed that my Meteors T-shirt was streaked with blood. It looked quite the part.

After the fracas in the underpass, Vince, Knocker and I finished off the half-dozen cans of Breaker in the bag and as we walked home past the Chells playing fields barely a person crossed our tracks. Despite the occasional burst of excitement in the town centre it was often possible to walk fairly long distances across town without seeing a soul. This was mainly due to the town's development corporation whose utopian vision ensured that cars and pedestrians are kept as far apart as possible through a combination of tunnels, bridges and a network of paths which spread across the town like tendrils. With this set-up, the notion of 'main' roads is almost entirely alien to the good folks of Stevenage as it is possible to get from place to place by a variety of routes, all of which are of a similar distance. Personally I find this part of New Town life the most appealing as it offers the opportunity to avoid a fair number of the town's low lifes along with the need to either ignore or rebuke the fairly frequent abuse which my hairstyle and dress sense often attract. Funnily, there is far less abuse directed my way when I am with the dozen or so other Stevenage Psychobillies that are my close friends but on my own I am a fairly legitimate target for mainstream morons and those who take their fashion tips from Simon Le Bon. Generally though it is a low-level annoyance and many of the town's other alternative types take a far more flack from the oiks, particularly the Goths, Heavy Metal followers and a trio of Gary Numan fans who sport black clothes, blonde hair and a touch of make-up.

As we got to the end of my street Vince and Knocker reminded me of our forthcoming trip to the Klub Foot, Psychobilly's mecca which could be found upstairs in a crumbling hotel on London's Hammersmith Broadway. Excitement levels were high as our previous visit had been a real tear-up with great bands, great wreckin' and a chance to peek at some of the scene's tastiest crumpet. Knocker had even got a blow-job that night in the toilets from some gypsy looking bird with crooked teeth and a massive Rockabilly quiff.

      This time we were hiring a van and a dozen of us were heading down to the capital. Vince in particular was keen to see some of the newer bands who would be playing and Knocker obviously believed that the trip would almost guarantee him another opportunity to get his helmet polished. Either way it was bound to be an unforgettable weekend.

We said our goodbyes and I walked up to my front door. My street was empty, a straight row of uniform council houses distinguishable only by their different coloured doors. Many a time I had returned home pissed and was rumbled by neighbours as I repeatedly jammed my key into their lock, unable to even spot my own front door in the line-up. As I slammed the door behind me I grabbed a jacket from the peg hooks on the wall and slipped it on in an attempt to cover up my blood-stained T-shirt. My mum spied me from the kitchen but after a brief flash of alarm had passed across her face she seemed to realise that I was in one piece and obviously decided to make no comment. I followed her into the living room where my dad was slouched on the couch watching 'Dempsey & Makepeace'. We made a little small talk and, despite finding the bird who played Makepeace a bit of a turn-on, I decided against sitting down with them and made my way up to my room.

From behind my big sister Yvonne's bedroom door I could hear the tinny electro-beat of one of her Soft Cell albums and the muffled sound of her and her friends gossiping. Despite the fact that they were all disco dollies who treated 'Smash Hits' with the same reverence as the bible, a few of her pals were real tasty sorts, particularly one called Pamela Donald who was a few years older than me - something that stimulated me even further. What with thoughts of firm-bosomed Pamela and that spicy blonde copper Makepeace I knew that a wank would be order at some time in the evening so I made a quick detour to the bathroom and pulled off a suitable length of bog roll. I always seemed to pull off too much on occasions like this but I was constantly worried that too little would involve me waddling back to the bog with my trousers and pants at my ankles in an attempt to mop up any remaining baby batter. Since I had discovered the art of non-stop knuckle shuffling in my early teens, our family went through more toilet paper than a battalion of squaddies suffering from dysentery.

I jammed the bog roll under my pillow, unlaced my boots and reached into my well-thumbed record collection. Bearing in mind our impending trip to London I sussed that a blast from 'Stomping At The Klub Foot' was in order. It did not seem so long ago that this album had been a real revelation to me, bringing The Guana Batz, Restless, The Sting-Rays and Thee Milkshakes into my home for the first time and I peered in awe at its cover which illustrated a venue crammed with Psychobillies. Though we were the minority in Stevenage, the Klub Foot seemed vast and populated almost entirely by the rockin' community. When we first got there it was nothing more than a crumbling, sweat-soaked ballroom full of punters like us but between those four blue walls it still felt like home.

As I listened to the album I felt a buzz of excitement knowing that the live recording of a third album was happening this coming Saturday and we were going to be there. The ticket was already pinned to my wall. Six bands and a chance to get a picture of our ugly mugs on the cover… sheer heaven. Before I settled down onto the bed I opened the window then sparked up a small one-skin joint that I had hidden in my jacket pocket. As side one eventually clicked off my stereo I was too chilled out to turn the album over and instead drifted into quiet contemplation. As I turned the events of the evening over in my mind I smiled contentedly. A fight, some booze, a joint and the opportunity to beat my bishop over the thought of Pamela Donald gyrating in a leotard just like Olivia Newton John in her 'Physical' video. Now that's what I call a Sunday night.

# Chapter 2
# The Psychobilly Disease

All through my early teenage years I had always been looking for something to belong to. The local nitwits pledged loyalty to their part of town and ruthlessly defended a street corner or a fucking park bench where they supped cider at the weekend. I could never see the point in that as I had no particular love for the estate I lived in, it was simply a place I went home to at night. Most folks seemed to be able to satisfy their tribal instinct to belong by following a football team but, again, that left me cold. I made half-hearted attempts to tie my colours to a team and as a lad I even bought a few copies of Shoot! and some Panini stickers but my soul was never really in it.

Music was the only thing that moved me. From an early age, Thursday nights in front of the TV watching Top Of The Pops was my religion. All through the 1970's I gawped and savoured a steady stream of Glam Rock, Disco, Soul, Reggae and mindless Pop music. As the decade progressed, every Sunday I would sit next to my Mum and Dad's music centre with two C90 tapes at the ready to record Radio One's Top 40 Countdown which I would then replay all week on my little hand-held cassette player with the single speaker.

When Punk came along everything changed - gradually. The history books would have it that Punk Rock had an immediate and seismic effect on the music business but even when The Sex Pistols were at their peak the likes of Olivia Newton John, Hot Chocolate and Wings were still cluttering up the Pop charts on a regular basis. Even though Stevenage was not a million miles from London's Kings Road the only sign of a Punk revolution in my town was a few geezers with tight trousers and short haircuts. Nonetheless, even at a tender age I sensed that something was happening but was frustrated as I struggled to find out what it was. As a ten year old my only supply of music came from the local Woolworths' record department. Even as a child I doubted that they had any more interest in music than they had for Mars Bars, especially when the nicotine-stained old hag behind the counter would ruthlessly stamp the cover of each 7" single with a hole punch just so that she could hang the records on a display board of metal pegs.

Over the next few years I took what I could get there and amongst the pile of mainstream shit that clogged the charts at the turn of the decade I unearthed a few diamonds from bands such as The Undertones, Darts, Stiff Little Fingers, UK Subs, Matchbox and The Stray Cats. Even then a pattern was emerging amongst my buying habits but I was ignorant to the fact that deep in London's musical underground Rockabilly and Punk were being welded together to create a hybrid of mythical proportions.

Buying records, wanking and attempting to get a grip on some of the local sorts more or less dominated my early teens. All through secondary school I drifted close to many street cults such as Punk, New Wave, Mod, Ska and even Heavy Metal but I was never committed to a single genre. I liked a bit of everything but kept it quiet. At home I could quite happily slip on a Twisted Sister album after a Secret Affair track but suspected few would share my enthusiasm for such a varied taste in music. Lines were sharply drawn at school and if you did not belong to the cliques of Punks, Skins, Mods and Heavy Rockers then you were nothing - which pretty much describes the entire period of my time at secondary school. Five years of undistinguished grades and passing friendships. Had my name not been on the register during that time then no one would have known I had been there.

It was somewhat ironic then that when I really began to enjoy school life was in my last term there. It was at a Christmas party in the home of one of my vague acquaintances that I first met Vince and Baz. I was sitting on the couch nursing a can of Strongbow and doing that thing where you catch the eye of some tasty girl, give her a little half-smile and a raise of the eyebrows and expect her to come over and stick her tongue down your throat. I later found out that this was a complete waste of fucking time and with Stevenage girls you had to do all the work, such as chatting them up and being a bit flash, before you even got near to giving them a sloppy kiss and getting a squeeze at their arse cheeks.

Baz and Vince plonked themselves down roughly on the couch next to me, shaking me out of my stupor and making me drop my can onto my lap. As I quickly struggled to avoid cider-soaked bollocks they both had a titter at my expense.

'You alright mate?' said Vince.

'Pissed yourself have you?' laughed Baz.

The two of them looked a little different to most of the bleached posers and shuffling Indie kids at the party. Baz had a spiky topped shock of natural blond hair that made him look like a pimply Billy Idol and Vince, with his greased-back barnet, seemed the type that had seen Grease one too many times and saw the Fonz as a real role model. We got talking though and they seemed like good guys. They were geezers with a bit of character, unlike many of the bland punters from school who I had spent my spare time with, often more by necessity than desire. They were supping a bit too and as I struggled to keep up with them, I began to get a bit more into the party spirit, especially when Baz slipped a copy of 'Friggin' In The Riggin'' onto the stereo and we attempted a three man can-can which resulted in Baz accidentally sticking his boot through the glass door of a trophy cabinet. As we attempted to clear up the broken glass and dented Crown Green Bowling statuettes another pissed-up party patron had taken a knife from the kitchen drawer and started threatening people in the hallway, which more or less brought the bash to a screeching halt. After that night I began to see more of Vince, Baz and their mates and my musical horizons were about to be stretched a little further.

Vince and Baz took me under their wing over the next few weeks as they started to turn up at my house with armfuls of records and began my re-education, introducing me to the likes of The Polecats, The Blue Cats and Crazy Cavan. It was all good stuff but the night that they brought over The Meteors' debut album changed everything. Listening to 'In Heaven' was like hearing all my favourite music all at once, it literally slapped me around the head. Not long after that I got a hold of 'Wreckin' Crew' and from then on my record collection got an overhaul. There was not much on offer in Stevenage but I got the train down to North London on occasional weekends and returned with whatever I could afford. Soon, all that was played in my room was The Sharks, King Kurt, The Ricochets, Skitzo, Frenzy and great compilations like 'Stomping at the Klub Foot' and 'Hell's Bent On Rockin''. My style was changing as well. Baz and Vince had both ditched their Punk and Ted hairstyles respectively and they now sported sharp flat-tops, cleanly shaved at the back and sides. It was not long before I was in the barber's chair demanding the same.

  We started to notice other flat-top types emerging around town and one Saturday we met four guys who were about our age as they sat on a bench in the town square, drinking cider and abusing passers by. Shane Nichols and Kev Harris were from Shephall, one of Stevenage's less desirable areas. They both had fairly long quiffs, missing teeth and a few scratchy, homemade tattoos but they were friendly blokes and always keen to talk about the Psychobilly scene. Their other Psychobilly mates were Stan Taylor, Jack Walker and Kenny Priest. Stan was a tall, skinny guy who had been kicked out of the army for some infringement but at least he already had his haircut sorted. Jack was a far more moody character. For a start he rarely answered to his Christian name and preferred only to be known as Knocker. He was a fairly big lump of a bloke, a bit of a rugby-playing type, and also a bit flash. His gear was always a little better than most of us and he really fancied himself as a ladies man. The rest of the guys welcomed us on board but Knocker seemed to withhold his judgement on us for some time.

Although Knocker was none too scrawny, Kenny Priest was your actual brick shithouse. He was not only tall but muscle-bound like Brian Jacks off of 'Superstars'. He had been working as a scaffolder for four years but I remembered him from school and even then he was a real hard nut. I had been a good few years below him and regularly saw him beating the shit out of people in the playground. He did not seem to seek out trouble but a guy of his size always attracted the attention of would-be hard men keen to gain some credibility. Most of them only gained sore bollocks and broken teeth.

Kenny had no recollection of me at school but he was friendly enough to Vince, Baz and I and seemed happy enough to spend time with anyone that Shane and Kev regarded as okay. Though he was fully into the style and music of Psychobilly, he originally came from the Rockabilly scene and it was obviously still his first love. Kenny's girlfriend Lynne and her friend Shona also hung about with us and eventually Shona and Stan became an item. They were the first Psychobilly girls that I had met and they looked great. Lynne had a massive black beehive-type quiff and Shona had an immaculately clipped short, blonde flat-top. They had fairly shapely bodies too but most of the time their figures were well disguised under tartan shirts and denims. They were no shrinking violets either and they would not hesitate to give any of us a slap if they thought we were out of order. The first time I saw them in action was a real eye opener as they set about three Disco chicks who saw fit to mock their Psychobilly style. Lynne even kicked one of the girls in the fanny, something I had never seen before or since.

After a few months the eleven of us were almost inseparable and even Knocker gradually warmed to us. Every weekend we were out drinking, either hanging around the streets with a carry-out or boozing in the local pubs. Stevenage even had its own alternative venue and we regularly went to gigs at the Bowes Lyon House. It was mostly Indie bands who played there but the local rockin' heroes were The Pharaohs and they often took to the stage at the Bowes. Seeing them was my first taste of a full-on Psychobilly band onstage. Although they peddled something closer to Rockabilly, I was gob-smacked by their performance and could not believe that they were a home-grown act who had also trod the boards at the Klub Foot. The best was yet to come though and a few weeks later we all travelled down to a club called Dingwalls in London to see The Meteors. The band were furious, the wrecking was fierce and the whole venue crackled with antagonism. I probably should have known better but I was drawn into the pit and pummelled senseless. After that, the whole evening was a blur but I will never forget the feeling of that first Meteors' gig.

After that night, the feeling of constantly bruised arms, and the occasional thump round the head, gained on various dance floors was the norm. The rest of my body got a fair workout as well. This usually took the form of the welcome sting of bruised knuckles, if we had a successful rumble, or the unwelcome throb of kicked bollocks and a sore face if we were on the losing side in a street fight or pub brawl. The very fact that we looked different to most of the town's characterless youths was more than enough to provoke a barney but as time moved on we also began to get, and give, back-up from a lot of the local Skins and Punks and we became less of an easy target. Either way I did not mind, I would rather be a Psychobilly and have something to fight for than just be a nothing and be ignored.

    Another part of my body that was getting a workout was my bell-end. Almost from the day I emerged from the barber's chair with my first flat-top I was attracting far more birds than I ever had. All through my later school years I enjoyed a few sporadic fumbles, dry runs and the odd poke at parties, school discos and the like but nothing serious. I eventually lost my virginity at sixteen to the daughter of my art teacher, while on a school trip. My technique had yet to blossom and it was no more than two pumps, a shiver and a shake. As far as I was concerned, the foreplay consisted of me pulling on the johnny bag. I am sure she had experimented with the full bunk-up a few times before as she must have had something to judge my poor technique against and I was never offered a rematch. The disappointment of my poor performance was matched however with a surge of relief that I had finally offloaded my virginity, tied a knot around it and flushed it down the lav.

    I got plenty practice in my early Psychobilly days as there was always spare crumpet circulating around our crew consisting of ex-girlfriends, Goth and Skin girls, local strumpets and even some of Knocker's cast-offs. Many a night I found myself behind the chippy with my trousers round my ankles or creaking the bedsprings on a stranger's bed at some house party. The whole experience left me in a spin. After years of keeping myself to myself I was now part of something. My social life was a whirl of booze, hash and speed. Now my nights could be spent hanging with my mates, perhaps sticking the boot into some cheeky ponce or slipping a length to some neighbourhood boiler but the most important thing was the soundtrack to it all - Psychobilly. The fighting I could take or leave and the regular shagging was an enjoyable sideline but going to gigs, buying records and discovering new bands was the real source of my happiness. Thank fuck I had met Baz and Vince at that party, otherwise I could have been doomed to lie wanking in my room and listening to Top 40 drivel for the remainder of my teenage years.

# Chapter 3
# Oi Thatcher! Up yours!

By the time I left school, some bright spark in the government had dreamt up the idea of press-ganging thousands of the nation's work-shy school leavers into the 'Youth Training Scheme' programme. Basically they jammed you into some menial labour job with an equally coerced employer who was driven purely by the fact that they did not have to pay you anything as the government would substitute your dole money for a minimal £25 a week 'training grant'. Even though my dad offered to help me follow in his footsteps as a painter & decorator and get me an apprenticeship, I was never really that interested in it and drifted onto the dole for a while before the YTS Gestapo got me in their sights and forced me to sign on the dotted line. I ended up working for the council and found myself in their sign making department, based in a small warehouse up on the Gunnels Wood industrial estate. It was not a bad job, knocking out street signs and banners, and my boss Bernie was a nice guy with some real Socialist leanings. He saw the YTS scheme as only slightly above slavery and for that reason he gave me a pretty easy time of it.

During my days there I also had a little sideline making number plates, particularly small custom sized ones for many of the town's bikers and scooterists. As well as cocking a blind eye to my use of company property as the basis of a small business, Bernie's attitude to time-keeping was also pretty broad-minded and he regularly let me skim the odd 15-30 minutes off my daily shift. On big occasions, such as my forthcoming jaunt to the Klub Foot, he was even more lenient so on the Friday before the event I was out the door at 2pm with my weekend gear packed. My 'holiday' clothes consisted of two T-shirts and an extra pair of jeans, all rolled together and jammed into a plastic carrier bag. Outside the factory was the shittiest looking transit van I had seen in a long time. It was a real rust-bucket with doors that looked as if they were held on with cable ties. It was parked right in the middle of the car park and blocking off most of our department's vans. I was about to go back in and let Bernie know when I recognised a figure in the trashcan on wheels. As I walked towards it I could see Baz in the passenger seat and Kenny Priest behind the wheel.

'You have got to be joking?' I said incredulously. 'Tell me this is not our transport down to the smoke?'

'What the fuck is wrong with it?' shouted Kenny seriously.

'It's a skip on wheels,' I said, and as I looked at it up close it definitely did not look any better.

'Look Harry' said Baz, 'Its Kenny's brother's and we got it dirt cheap…'

'… dirt's the word,' I interrupted.

Baz continued, '… but it keeps the cost down. Its only gonna cost us £4 each, and that includes the diesel.'

He waited for a response but I was still checking out the relic. 'C'mon get in,' shouted Kenny. 'We're having a night at Shane and Kev's then leaving straight from there in the morning.'

I pulled open the sliding door at the side of the van to reveal an even worse state of decay; old building materials, empty plastic cups, fish & chip wrappers and more covered the floor.

I found it hard to hide my disgust, 'Oh for fuck's sake.'

'Get in you poof,' yelled Kenny and began the long, complicated combination of key turning, accelerator stomping and choke pulling which was required to stoke some life into the beast.

As I stood at the back, moaning about the lack of seating space, Kenny managed to spark some life into the vehicle and immediately lurched the van forward sending me flying into a half-empty cement bag and pile of stained dustsheets which lay near the back doors. Here we go I thought, as I wiped the dust from my T-shirt while Baz and Kenny laughed like drains. The weekend starts here.

Where I lived was not exactly Beverly Hills but Shane and Kev's flat was in one of the worst streets in Stevenage, if not in the whole of Hertfordshire. In some parts of Shephall their idea of garden furniture was a burnt-out sofa, empty beer cans and the odd dirty needle. We managed to park near their gaff but, thankfully, the van looked too fucked-up to interest even the most desperate tea-leaf. When we got inside we realised that almost everyone else was there and they had already started boozing and passing round some joints. Shane and Kev had obviously been at it all day and were pretty wasted. Knocker, Stan and Stevie had only just arrived before us and were just into their first few cans. Kenny threw himself down on the couch next to Lynne and Shona.

'Alright hot pants,' Kenny said as he gave Lynne a kiss. 'Did you get my booze?'

'It's down at the side of the couch. Did you get the whizz?'

Kenny slapped the breast pocket of his shirt, 'No problem Hun.'

'Alright Harry!' shouted Vince. He was sat at a table at the back of the room, attempting to build a water-cooled bong from an empty plastic drinks bottle and a pen.

I noticed that Knocker had already made himself comfortable on the couch next to Elizabeth Castle, the local bike. She was a right skank and had been up to unmentionables almost all the way through secondary school. That is where she gained her nickname, 'Bike Shed Betty', tossing off a variety of schoolboys for money and cigarettes. She lived nearby and made quite regular appearances at Shane and Kev's house, often just to leech some of their booze and drugs but occasionally for a bunk-up. They had both shagged her, on different occasions but once they had indulged in a 'two-up' although they claimed that their balls started banging together at one point, which they felt was a bit gay, so they packed it in. Regardless of her pedigree, Knocker seemed keen to make a move probably because the only other two girls in the room were Lynne and Shona.

As the evening progressed Knocker somehow persuaded Elizabeth to pull out his cock and blow him off right where they sat together on the couch. As she got to work on his pole I looked around the room and only Vince and I seemed to be raising our eyebrows in silent shock. No one else seemed particularly fazed and I figured that it must be one of her regular party pieces. Stevie obviously also fancied getting into the swing of it and with a notion to be second in line for her sucking services he shouted across the room.

'Hey Betty! Where's my share?'

Without even blinking, Elizabeth removed Knocker's prick from her mouth and pointed the swollen weapon in Stevie's direction as if she was offering him a chance to suck on it. Stevie went bright red and slouched down in his chair swigging deeply from his beer can.

'That's not what I meant.'

Everyone took great pleasure in his embarrassment and near pissed themselves laughing, apart from Knocker who guided Elizabeth's lips back on to his throbber.

Apart from the live sex show, the evening was pretty uneventful. Everyone was excited about our trip to Hammersmith and seemed to be saving themselves for it. We carried on supping though but gradually some folks started to fall asleep. I felt tired myself but just as I was settling down deeper into my chair I noticed a mischievous glint in Shane and Kev's eyes. They were notorious for shaving anyone who crashed out at their flat with their electric clippers. Eyebrows and hair were the standard targets but occasionally they got a bit more creative and once I had woken up in their living room with my trousers undone and most of my pubes on the carpet. My balls were itching for about a week. It was rumoured that they even shaved Elizabeth's pussy completely bare after she spent a night in Shane's bed but I do not imagine it really bothered her. My hair was looking pretty smart and I did not fancy them fucking about with it before my return visit to the Klub Foot so I did a little line of speed which I found among the empty beer cans which littered the table next to me then cracked open my final can and waited for Shane and Kev to fall asleep.

# Chapter 4

# Klub Foot Stompin' - Wham! Bam! Thank-you Pam!

I woke up about 7am and the first thing I did was check that my quiff and my eyebrows were intact. I was not that bothered about losing the hair on my pubes but I had a feel down there anyway and everything felt okay. As I gained full consciousness I started to feel cramp in my legs so I struggled out of my chair and began jigging around to ease the pain. I did not realise that Stan and Shona had bedded down on the floor close to me and I accidentally stomped on Stan's ankle. He woke up with a yell.

'Fucking hell Harry! An alarm call would have done.'

'Sorry mate,' I said as I attempted to suppress a giggle.

'Fuck off!' he replied and snuggled up against Shona again under a sleeping bag.

I could now feel both legs again so I stepped over a few other bodies on the floor and made my way to the bog. The first piss of the day always seems to look like weak lager, it even has a head on it. Knocker and Elizabeth Castle had fallen asleep in the bath with only a worn bed sheet covering them. I did not know what they had been up to but I could take a guess as one of her bare, spotty butt cheeks was peeking from beneath the cover.

I went into the kitchen and found Kenny and Lynne huddled round the cooker trying to light their fags from a ring on the electric cooker. I passed my lighter to Lynne without speaking.

'Cheers love,' she said.

Although Lynne was only a few years older than me, she always spoke to most of us like a mother figure. For this reason, despite the fact that she was pretty tasty, I never really fancied her. I had had a few wanks over the thought of Shona riding my flagpole but generally I just thought of both of them as part of the group. Also, I did not fancy the thought of facing extensive facial reconstruction surgery if Kenny caught me looking the wrong way at his bird.

'You ready for the Klub Foot Powell?' croaked Kenny as he exhaled his first lungful of smoke.

'Fucking right mate. Glad my barnet is still in one piece. Shane and Kev are a bit handy with them clippers some times.'

'Too fucking right,' he laughed as he tapped the oven door with his boot, 'That's why I hid them in here.'

'Are you going to tell them?' I asked.

'Not fucking likely. They can find them next time they fancy a plate of oven chips. They're too sneaky with those fucking things anyway. I told them that if they touch me with them I'll leave them like a pair of Kojaks.'

Lynne was poking around the kitchen looking for tea bags. She found a box but it was empty. As she threw the box in the bin she took a sharp intake of breath and screwed her face up.

'It stinks in here. Couple of pigs.'

'I see Knocker made himself comfy,' I said.

Kenny sneered, 'He don't care where he puts it.'

'That Castle is a right dog,' added Lynne. 'She was asking Knocker if she could come with us down to London. Why the fuck would she want to come to the Klub Foot. Saturday nights at the Long Ship is where she usually plies her trade.'

Stan and Shona joined us. Stan was limping and slapped the back of my head as he walked past.

'Cheers for the wake up,' he said sarcastically.

'Any tea?' asked Shona sleepily.

'Nothing,' said Lynne, 'These two live like a pair of fucking hoboes.'

Stan opened the fridge and exclaimed, 'Aha. Here is breakfast,' as he pulled four cans of Breaker from the fridge. He cracked one open, took a deep draught from it then passed it to me. I took a sip and went to pass it back.

'C'mon,' he shouted as he pushed the can towards me. 'Get stuck in. We've got some good rockin' tonight.'

As I took another sip I noticed that his limp had faded as he grabbed Shona and tried to jive her around the room. With Shona still in his grip he grabbed the can back and took another drink. He could see that the rest of us were still in a stupor so he started a bit of light wrecking around the kitchen, bumping into us and prodding us gently with his fists.

'C'mon, c'mon,' he said as he made for the living room. As I glugged down some more of the can I could hear him shouting.

'Right you lazy bastards, get up. We're going to the Klub Foot.'

Despite Stan's rousing early morning call, it took ages to get everyone up and ready to go. Shona and Lynne went to the local shop then tried to rouse everyone back to consciousness with an offer of tea and bacon baps. By 1pm we were in the van and off down the A1. Shona and Lynne were upfront with Kenny while the rest of us roughed it in the back. Knocker had even managed to shake off Elizabeth.

'That Castle is a right slut,' said Stevie as he questioned Knocker, 'What the fuck were you up to last night?'

Knocker smirked, 'You know me, I never pass up the chance to drop a load.'

'Yeh,' said Vince nudging Stevie, 'But you were keen enough to get her lips around your tip.'

'Alright, alright. I just thought if it was on offer I'd have a bit,' said Stevie as he obviously wished that he had kept his mouth shut.

Stan laughed, 'She could probably have given you both a blow job at once.'

'No way,' protested Stevie. 'I wouldn't want my bell end touching his. You don't know where it's been.'

'Up a bird's crack,' said Knocker smugly, 'And that's where it will be again tonight.'

From this low point , the conversation degenerated even further until Lynne got sick of the low-brow chat and yelled at us.

'Pack it in you fucking perverts.'

As we passed beyond the M25 into the heart of the capital we began drinking more earnestly as the excitement began to build. I was buzzing, as the two 'Stomping At The Klub Foot' albums were so legendary that I could not believe we were going to witness the recording of a third volume. I jabbed my hand into my pocket in a brief moment of panic and only relaxed when I pulled out my ticket.

'Has everyone got these?' I said as I waved the red ticket.

There were a few more panicked fumblings amongst the crew but eventually everyone confirmed that they were sorted.

As soon as we came off the North Circular Road I started to spot other Psychobillies on the streets and the closer we got to Hammersmith their numbers increased. Even though it was only mid-afternoon just being outside the Klub Foot was a huge part of the experience; mingling with other Psychobillies, checking out a wide variety of hairstyles and looking for familiar faces and fresh crumpet was hugely enjoyable in itself.

'Clarendon up ahead,' yelled Kenny and we all leaned forward to get a peek out of the windscreen.

Even in the daylight the Clarendon's neon sign glowed red and under the canopy which covered the main entrance was a small army of Psychobillies. They spilled out onto the pavements at either side and some were scattered on the main road. The metal barriers which lined the pavements were almost totally obscured by the huge number of bequiffed punters who sat, stood or leant against them. Even from the van I could tell that the atmosphere was electric.

'Right Priest,' shouted Knocker, 'Get this fucking thing parked. I'm ready for it.'

We all felt the same. After what seemed like an age, and on a route that seemed to take us away from the Klub Foot, Kenny finally settled on a parking space that suited his requirements. As we piled out of the van and started walking, Kenny shouted at us.

'Don't forget! We're parked at North End Road.'

None of us were listening.

All the drink that we brought with us in the van was long gone so we replenished our supply at the nearest off-licence, just enough to neck until we got into the venue. As we turned a corner The Clarendon was back in view and it looked busier than ever. A lot of the London punters who were regulars there, either upstairs in the main hall or at the smaller downstairs 'Broadway' venue, were fairly blasé about the Klub Foot's significance as the centre of the Psychobilly universe. For anyone beyond the M25 though it was almost mythical. There were few places in the country that could draw a Psychobilly crowd from across the UK. There was a big crew from Bristol, Brummies, Geordies, some Welsh folks and even a few Jocks. People from all points of the compass outside London knew that this was the place to come for Psychobilly and outside the venue this was evident. The crowd was a swirling mass of wild hairstyles and varied accents. The buzz was so overwhelming that I had to stop myself from staring slack jawed at everyone and maintain some charade that this was just another day's rockin' for a Psychobilly like me. All though we stayed loosely together everyone was shouting out to people that they knew from other gigs which we had attended and Knocker had already started to snake his way around some of the girls in the queue.

When the doors opened, the crowd on the street started to flood through the creaky entrance, eventually leaving the pavement once more to the harassed locals and tut-tutting old folks who were either bemused, angered or horrified by this regular invasion of rowdy rockers. As I climbed the steps to the first floor I could feel a real sense of excitement which seemed to cling to me like a pair of sweaty underpants. When we entered the hall it was already almost full and behind us the punters kept coming. Upstairs the stage was empty but the DJ was already spinning some rocking tracks.

'This is the place,' I said to Stan in anticipation.

'Too right Powell, I'm fucking ready for it,' he replied.

Luckily I was pretty pissed already as the bar was almost five bodies deep and pretty hard to get to but Kenny passed round a half-bottle of Vodka that he had got Lynne to smuggle in. I took a sip but I did not need much more booze to get me high. Just being there was the biggest buzz. We all stood together for a bit and chatted amongst ourselves and with a few punters nearby that we had met at gigs before. Soon the hall was crammed, elbow to elbow. Nowhere else had I seen more Psychobillies in one place. This felt more like home than anywhere. I thought about wading my way through the crowd for a piss but then the lights began to dim.

Although it was the middle of Summer, the night air

felt ice cold on my sweat-soaked body as I squeezed through the main doors of the Clarendon onto the street. The Klub Foot crowd hit the pavements of Hammersmith like a bomb, flooding out of the venue screaming, shouting and singing. I was pushed along until I managed to find space to stand in a shop doorway. I could feel my arms starting to throb steadily as they had been tenderised under a wave of fists during the bouts of wrecking which I had attempted. My arse was also sore and soaked in sticky booze as I had been knocked to the ground so many times. I felt great though, it had been a marvellous gig. My mind was whizzing but I gradually managed to piece what I had just witnessed back together. I could not quite remember how it all progressed but I did recall how it was a game of two halves. Slick but fearsome Rockabilly from Rochee & The Sarnos, The Wigsville Spliffs and The Caravans and all-out Psychobilly fury from Torment, The Coffin Nails and Batmobile.

    I have to admit that although I enjoyed the Rockabilly sets, it was during these parts of the gig that I took time to go for a piss, attempt to get served at the bar or chat with my mates about how well the gig was going. That was if I could find them, the crowd was so tight that it was almost impossible to stay in one place without getting edged along so often that when I returned to where I thought we had been congregated there was no one there. It did not make any difference though as when the Psychobilly bands were on I was either in the wrecking pit or deep inside the tightly packed crowd watching the action onstage.

       'Powell, over here!'
    I could hear Knocker's voice but could not see him until he broke through the crowd and joined me in the doorway.
       'What a fucking gig,' he gasped. 'Where are the

rest of them?'

'No idea mate,' I replied, 'I haven't seen anyone since The Coffin Nails were on.'

'Are you alright? That wrecking was fierce mate,' said Knocker.

'Yeh, but my arse is black and blue, I got knocked down that many times.'

'Well I'll tell you. Its my balls that are blue. I was chatting to some little sort in there and she was well up for it. She even stroked my tool through my jeans and then her fucking boyfriend appeared after Batmobile had finished. I've got to get a shag tonight mate, I'm not going back to that van with a hard-on.'

'What do you want to do then? Everyone's clearing out.'

'Hold on,' Knocker shouted across to a geezer in the crowd. 'Nobby! Over here.'

A couple of guys that I recognised from a gig at Reading came over.

'Fucking great gig. What you up to now?' said Knocker to them.

'There's a party at Goldhawk Road. You up for it?' said one of them.

'Is there going to be some birds there?' asked Knocker.

'There should be some crumpet,' replied the geezer. 'The bloke whose house it is, is a roadie for one of the bands. Those dirty bastards have always got some spare around.'

'What about the rest of them?' I asked Knocker.

'Fuck it,' he replied, 'The van will still be there in the morning. I need to get my nuts emptied.'

I saw Kenny and Lynne pass by and grabbed them then told them of our plan but they were keen to get some food then get a decent space in the van to pitch their sleeping bag. We said our goodbyes and Kenny warned us all not to forget where the van was or we would find ourselves walking back to Stevenage. I had no idea where Goldhawk Road was but it certainly sounded better than going back to that skanky Transit for a kip. We followed the Reading boys away from the venue as the crowds drifted apart and the glowing red Clarendon sign faded into the distance.

After walking what seemed like miles through the back streets of London we finally found the party in a cramped basement flat. Almost as soon as we got through the door, Knocker shot off like a terrier on heat in search of female company. I ended up in the kitchen, nursing a can of booze that I was offered and chatting to some Scotsmen who were also coming down from the euphoria of the gig and similarly had no fucking idea where they were. I sat on a hard plastic chair next to the bin and eventually nodded off to sleep.

I awoke some hours later with a cold, damp feeling over my bollocks. Thankfully I had not pissed myself but I had dropped the half-full can of lager in my lap. I found a manky tea towel and attempted to rub myself dry but the booze had soaked straight through to my pants and beyond. The party was dead now and as I attempted to find the bog I had to step over the mass of snoring and farting bodies which littered the living room floor. After finding the hall cupboard and a bedroom, I finally located the room in the house most suitable for the emptying of the bladder.

As I walked into the bathroom I almost collided with Knocker who was standing near the door. It took me a few seconds to realise but it then hit me that he was actually naked from the waist down and in the middle of banging a girl who sported a rather fetching purple quiff. She had her back to him and was clutching the sides of the sink while panting wildly as he entered her from behind in something of a variation on the 'doggy style'.

'For fuck's sake!' I said in a mixture of surprise

and disgust. 'Don't you lock the bog door when you are busy?'

As I moved to walk out the bathroom Knocker grabbed my arm firmly, 'No Harry. Hold on… nearly done.'

Before I could leave he gave the girl two powerful thrusts and that final shiver that usually accompanies the emptying of the bollocks. As he withdrew his sagging member and reached to the floor for his trousers he spanked the girl playfully on one of her butt cheeks and delivered his post-coital sweet talk.

'Cheers love.'

The girl was furious. She gathered up her clothes quickly and shoved past me out of the bathroom while shouting back at Knocker.

'Fucking arsehole!'

Knocker laughed as he sat down on the toilet seat and began to lace up his boots.

'What's happening then?' he said nonchalantly.

'You had your share then?' I asked.

'Oh yes,' he said with a similar sense of satisfaction to that of someone who has just enjoyed a good meal or a posh cigar.

'Who was she?' I queried.

'Oh, just some bird.' Knocker stood up and started to walk into the hallway, 'C'mon, this party's dead.'

We stepped over a few bodies who were crashed out in the hall and as we left the house the sun was starting to rise above the rooftops of the tightly-terraced houses. There was no one around and as a relatively rare visitor to the capital it was unusual to see the place so peaceful in the daylight. As I took in this rare period of calm in the city that never sleeps Knocker punctuated the silence with the words I really did not want to hear.

'Harry. Where the fuck are we?'

By the time we got back to van, after wandering the streets like a pair of tramps for what seemed like ages, the rest of the crew were waiting for us. As we opened the side door the smell of dried sweat, stale beer and kebabs almost made me heave.

'Where the fuck have you been?' shouted Kenny. He was pretty angry. 'We've been waiting here for fucking ages.'

'It's only eight 'o' clock, keep your hair on,' said Knocker. 'If you had parked nearer the Klub Foot we might have been able to find the fucking thing. We've been walking about since sunrise.'

'Well get in then,' growled Kenny, 'Let's get fucking moving.'

'Hold on mate,' said Stan as he stuck his head out of the van and puked on the pavement.

'You dirty bastard, get away from me,' shrieked Shona as she got out of the van quickly.

Stan's puking woke everyone else up and they all shuffled onto the street, shaking themselves, spitting and lighting up their first fag of the day. Knocker insisted that I back up the story of his bathroom bunk-up and I grudgingly went along with it, admitting that although I never really saw her face she did seem pretty tasty. We talked about our night at the Klub Foot and everyone seemed to have felt much the same buzz I had experienced. Any thrill was long gone now though and after some more coughing, farting and stretching we decided that it was time for us homesick souls to make it back to the concrete canyons of Stevenage.

The hangovers did not last long and before we had even broke through North London we stopped at a greasy spoon for a nosh up. This coincided with the pub across the street opening its doors as we left the café, so naturally we nipped in for a hair of the dog. This led to a few more, a short drive further up the road to another boozer and before I knew it we were being kicked out of a pub on the outskirts of Stevenage at midnight.

After our all day booze session I was knackered, smelly and tired when Kenny pulled the van up to my house around 1am. In my mind I was already working out the nature of the sick call I was about to make to Bernie in the morning. As I slipped my key into the front door I noticed that the lights in the front room were still on. My folks did not usually stay up this late, even at weekends, but then I remembered that they were away for a few days and Yvonne and I had an empty. Even though I had been away it made no difference to me anyway as there was no way I would invite all my mates round for a booze-up. When I remember the state which we left some houses in after parties there was no way I would bring it into my home. Finding cling film over my own toilet and a shit in my sock drawer was not my idea of fun, although I did find it hilarious when it happened to someone else.

There was not much noise coming from inside but as I stood at the bottom of the stairs I could hear a bit of muffled giggling from one of the bedrooms. I noticed a pair of some bloke's slip-on shoes on the floor and a horrible poser's blue leather jacket hanging over the banister so I assumed that my sister was 'entertaining' some poor sod up in her bedroom. The thought gave me a little cold shiver so I thought I would crash out in front of the TV instead of listening to my sister do the knee-bone knock for the rest of the night.

On the living room stereo someone had left some awful weepy Spandau Ballet track playing and as I made a direct move to rip the needle off the record I noticed Pamela Donald was curled up on the couch and sobbing quietly. Even with wet mascara giving her the panda eyes she still looked pretty spectacular.

'Sorry Pam,' I said, 'Were you listening to that?'

'Yes,' she answered in a croaky voice, 'Could you leave it on?'

'No problem,' I said as I made a move for my Dad's old chair.

'You can sit here if you want,' said Pamela as she patted the chair next to her.

I took my jacket off and kicked a few empty cider bottles accidentally as I plonked myself down next to her. Through the tears, I could see that she was a bit pissed but she still looked stunning. She had kicked off her white high heels and all she had on were a pair of white footless tights, a tiny yellow ra-ra skirt and a tight lemon coloured T-shirt. Her breasts looked firm to the point of bursting and I was not even sure if she had a bra on or if it was only the tightness of her top was supporting them.

'So how was the party then?' I asked.

She paused for a moment to let out a little half-sob then blurted out, 'It was a fucking disaster.'

Pamela's folks were from somewhere near Glasgow but although she had moved to Stevenage when she was just a tot she still had a little overtone of 'jockness' in her accent that was pretty cute.

'Barry Fry and his friend came over, just for a drink and a bit of a laugh y'know,' she continued.

Oh yeh, I thought, more like a double bunk-up with some bastard dropping his seed on my mum and dad's bed… or worse still, mine.

'So where are they now?' I asked.

She motioned upstairs, 'His friend Derek is upstairs but Barry has dumped me. He fucking dumped me Harry.'

I found the idea of anyone dumping Pamela pretty hard to imagine but Fry was a flash bastard and one of Stevenage's top posers. He drove a red Ford Capri and was always hanging about the school gates surrounded by a gaggle of dim-witted schoolgirls. Supposedly he had been Pamela's boyfriend for a couple of years but I had seen him driving around town on many occasions with all manner of skanks and under-agers.

Pamela was sobbing uncontrollably and I thought about putting a comforting arm round her shoulder but decided against such an obvious move.

'So what happened then?' I asked, attempting to adopt a concerned tone even though I was pretty chuffed that she was once again a free agent.

She wiped her eyes with an old tea towel that lay on the couch. 'Oh, he gave me some shit about me getting too serious. I think he's seeing someone else.'

I stifled a giggle, as he was probably lining up a bunch of local slappers right now in the bushes at Box Wood Nature Reserve on the edge of town.

'You shouldn't worry about it Pam, you're a good looking girl. Its early days yet. What are you? 20?'

She turned round to face me slightly and her knee brushed lightly against my thigh. Even that gentle touch started off a little stiffening in my trouser region. I reached for a bottle of cider that stood on the coffee table.

'C'mon have another drink.'

She put the bottle to her lips and took a deep swig. Her eyes were starting to dry. 'Too good for him aren't I?' she said, laughing slightly as she passed me the bottle.

'Yeh,' I agreed, 'You're better off with the flash bastard.'

She looked a little shocked and for one brief moment I thought she was about to slap my face, or tell me to fuck off, but all she did was let out a little half-hearted laugh as she stared at the floor.

'Sup up lass,' I said in my best 'oop North' accent as I attempted to lighten the atmosphere with a low-rent comedy impression while I thrust the cider back in her direction.

She took another swig and looked straight at

me. 'You know you're not as big an arsehole as your sister makes out.'

'Why? What has she been saying?' I said in mock indignation.

'Not much' said Pamela, 'Just that you wank all the time and constantly listen to Punk Rock and Teddy Boy music.'

'It's Psychobilly,' I said but knew instantly that it had fallen on deaf ears. 'What do you listen to?' I pointed to the stereo where Tony Hadley was still bleating. 'Not that old shite all the time?'

'No, I like lots of stuff.'

'Like what?' I persisted.

'ABC, Heaven 17, The Style Council, eh…'

I could see she was struggling. 'C'mon, tell the truth. Chart stuff?'

She blew a gentle parp from her lips and gave up. 'I don't really listen to music much.'

'Too busy keeping beautiful?' I said, laying on a sudden burst of charm with a fucking trowel. A statement like that would probably have got me glassed, or soaked with snakebite at the very least, if I had tried that weak chat-up line with most Psychobilly ladies but it seemed to quite tickle Pamela. Poser birds were obviously used to that sort of slimy chat and she reacted coyly.

'You think I'm beautiful then do you?'

'Not bad,' I said jokily as I felt a rush of blood to my helmet.

She punched me gently, 'Cheeky sod.'

I offered the cider bottle back to her and slyly moved my seating position to shield my emerging hard-on a bit. She took a deep draught from the bottle and passed it back.

'So what about you then? Have you got anyone at the moment?'

'Not really. Y'know, a few girls that hang about with us. I meet birds at gigs, nothing serious.'

'Like Lynne Spence and her friends? I remember her from school. She was scary,' said Pamela.

'Yeh, that's them. Lynne's going out with my mate Kenny. Kenny Priest?'

'So no one special?' she asked and bit her bottom lip tenderly.

'Not really,' I said as my dick tried to force its way through my fly. 'Why? Would it make any difference?'

'Not really,' she said and leaned forward slightly.

Bingo! Lip-on-lip action with Pamela Donald. I was fucking tingling all over. We slid down onto the couch, locked together with our tongues darting into each other's mouths. I slid my hands frantically onto her arse and squeezed her cheeks then slid my mitts up to her warm, full breasts with a real urgency. It was as if my mind was telling me that this was too good to be true and I had better get a good feel before she changed her mind. She was far from having second thoughts though and her hands moved down to loosen my studded belt. My Elvis buckle popped off like a dream and her smooth hand pulled down my zip and thrust into my underpants in search of my hard rod. Within seconds we were naked, although I could not be fucked taking the time to unlace my Doc Martens so I just jammed my trousers and pants down as far as I could over my ankles. I took a brief second to look at her beautiful naked body beneath me before I moved on top of her and slid my poker into her juicy lovebox.

Some of the more disastrous shags I had experienced were often no more than two pumps and a shiver but whether it was a result of my all-day alcohol intake or the fact that bunking-up Pamela had been such a surprise, even after some vigorous rumpo I was a long way from the vinegar strokes and I could see that Pamela was enjoying my firm, steady thrusting. Flushed with confidence, and still in some shock that I was bonking one of the hottest girls in town, I began to vary my technique and flipped between fast pounding strokes and slowly grinding against her, pushing her sweet, firm butt cheeks deep into the upholstery of our wildly creaking couch. She gripped me tightly and I could feel her hot breathe on my neck in little pants, as if she was uttering some foul but inaudible oaths.

Suddenly she sat up on the couch and pushed me backwards and for a few dreadful seconds I thought she had sobered up and learnt the error of her ways. Thankfully, she was just changing position and as I sat bolt upright on the couch she gripped my bell-end and lowered herself onto my cock. As she straddled me, she leant back slightly and her wonderful, firm knockers jiggled in front of my eyes. This was just too much and I felt that I was definitely on the home stretch. I thought for a few seconds about those delaying tactics that I had read about in a copy of Fiesta but I was too far gone. Gripping her arse firmly with both hands I pulled her body down onto my lap. She reacted by bouncing even more frantically on my throbbing member. We were locked together and as she started to let out increasingly sharp little yelps I could feel her warm love juice flowing over my pole. It was all too much and I delivered my creamy payload with such a force that my whole body stiffened and I thrust my body back so sharply that the back of my skull cracked against the wall behind the couch. Pamela's breathing grew easy as she rocked gently on my lap, seemingly squeezing every last bit of life out of my rapidly wilting cock. I lay back more gently this time, closed my eyes and drifted off into a tingling ecstatic sleep.

'You dirty bastard,' yelled Yvonne as she ripped open the curtains, sending shards of sunlight into my eyes.

It took a little time to get my head together but

as I roused myself from my deep sleep I realised that my sister, and her smugly smiling bedmate Derek Carter, were standing amongst the empty cans and booze bottles which were littered across the floor of our living room. As my befuddled mind began to clear a little more I also realised that I was completely naked with only my pants and trousers gathered in a tangle round my ankles. My knob had flopped against my thigh like an old tramp; wrinkled and damp.

'Is this what happens when mum and dad are away?' yelled Yvonne. 'You sit up wanking all night.'

Had I been in a better position and had my head together I could have hit straight back at her with the accusation that she was turning her bedroom into a twenty-four hour knocking shop but all I could come up with was a stuttered, 'But I wasn't… I didn't…'

As I looked around frantically to Pamela for support I soon sussed that she was long gone. Shoes, bag, jacket… the lot. Carter was chuckling away to himself and I new that I would not hear the last of this. With a mix of embarrassment and anger I quickly pulled up my trousers, got off the couch and pushed past them both as I left the room.

Yvonne shouted after me, 'Pervert!', and before I reached the bottom of the stairs I realised that for some reason that fucking Spandau Ballet song was still playing on the music centre.

# Chapter 5

# Boots, Bottles and Blades

The Friday after the Klub Foot was a big comedown in many ways. After witnessing a live event, that we all felt was already legendary, combined with a party afterwards and a piss-up on the way home in the van it had been a memorable weekend. Then it was made even more unforgettable when I returned home and got that surprise bunk-up with Pamela Donald. It seemed unlikely that Friday night in a Stevenage boozer could come anyway close to matching the whole experience. There was certainly no glimpse of another session with Pamela. I passed her in the hall during the week, when she was visiting my sister, she could barely look at me and only mumbled hello as she went into my sister's room. Nonetheless, I had no regrets. I would not have minded another poke at her but at the end of the day she was a disco dolly and we had nothing in common. I would, however, wank off to the memory of that night many times in the oncoming weeks.

The Coach was a pub which we frequented occasionally as, despite being a pretty mainstream boozer, it was one of the few ale houses that would serve us without question and did not adhere to any ridiculous 'dress code'. Many of the other drinking dens in the town were attempting to go down the wine bar / disco route and the last thing they wanted was a dozen or so herberts with 'funny' hair, ripped denims and steel-toe capped boots. The irony was that most of the times when we went out locally we were just after the opportunity to drink beer, have a laugh and chase crumpet. The smartly dressed George Michael lookalikes who frequented the trendiest watering holes were often far more likely to carve you up with a Stanley knife. I noticed a mob like that as I entered the pub. There were six of them huddled round a table near the bar, all laughing too loudly at their own jokes while throwing a few stares at my mates.

Near the back of the bar, at the fag machine, were Knocker, Stevie, Stan, Vince and Stan's older brother Bernie, a hulking skinhead who occasionally hung around with us. Stan and Stevie were already glaring back at the geezers but I just did not feel like rolling around the car park with a bunch of lairy lager louts so I tried to steer the conversation round to some reminiscing about our great time at the Klub Foot. Despite wanting to talk about the bands we had seen Knocker was still going on about his bunk-up in the bathroom at the party and I reluctantly backed up his story after he consistently badgered me to tell the guys what I had witnessed. To be fair I could almost forgive his relentless boasting as, although my memory was addled by booze and lack of sleep, she had seemed a pretty good looking girl. I doubted if he had any possibility of a rematch though after he had so bluntly dismissed her after their shag. It seemed more likely that she would have a good slap for him should their paths ever cross again.

Despite successfully turning the conversation round to the subject of sex, the poisonous atmosphere seeping from the six moustachioed posers across the bar was still drifting over to our table. Yet again, these knumbskulls could not get over our Psychobilly style and out of everyone else in the boozer it was us that had attracted their attention. Vince and Bernie had been doing some detective work at the bar and as they returned with the drinks they informed us that the geezers were from Slough and were spending the night in Stevenage as part of some football related trip. I noticed that Stan and Stevie were already starting to stock pile some empty beer bottles under the chair so I steeled myself for what seemed like an inevitable brawl. After half an hour though, things still had not kicked off and while the half-dozen wankers were still caning lager and shouting loudly, their interest in us seemed to have faded and they were no longer trying to stare us out. As things were starting to relax again, I realised that my bladder was getting a bit of a stretching and made my way to the bog.

      Although most boozers in town had those tiny, two piss-pot khazis the toilets at The Coach were unusually spacious with almost a whole wall of rust-stained urinals and four cubicles. As I let a steamy piss rattle against the metal I heard two voices and as I glanced at the doorway I saw two of the London geezers who had been sizing us up in the bar. I also noticed Vince behind them and as nothing much seemed to be up I continued to drain my bladder. Without warning, one of the half-wits pushed my head against the wall. I was stunned for a moment and then I felt my own warm piss trickle down my leg. Without really thinking I quickly pushed my knob back in my jeans then turned and landed my fist straight into the geezer's smirking face. Vince and the other guy were already rolling around on the toilet floor. Vince growled heavily and delivered short punches to his opponent's face in a bid to make him loosen the choke hold on his throat. My attacker seemed pretty witless and my single punch had sent him toppling backwards into a cubicle, leaving him momentarily sitting on the bog seat and attempting to get to his feet. Either I had the knuckle power of Terry McCann or he had a glass jaw and, suspecting the latter, I moved forward quickly to take advantage of his dazed state. Holding on to each side of the cubicle I stamped wildly at him with my boot in an attempt to prevent him getting to his feet. My Doc Marten rained down on his chest, his thigh and finally his chin but before I could finish the job two pairs of hands grabbed me from behind and threw me against the wall. Pain shot through my body and I crumpled onto the deck. I had just enough time to see at least eight more bodies burst into the gents before I had to curl up under the flurry of kicks which were aimed at me. Obviously the six guys at the bar had some more friends and it sounded as if Vince was getting the same treatment as me. I realised that if we stayed where we were, he and I were going to get seriously fucked over.

I made a lunge for the door and screamed out to Knocker and Stan before I was dragged back, subjected to an avalanche of punches and beaten to the floor once again. I was almost seeing dark spots of unconsciousness form in my eyes when I heard a scream from Knocker as he, Stan, Stevie and Bernie finally crashed through the door and all hell broke loose amongst the porcelain and pissed-on floor tiles.

As the toilet was so large there was plenty of room for a tear-up and immediately a full-scale brawl began. The guys who had been pummelling me obviously saw my friends as a more threatening proposition and they moved towards Knocker and the rest of my flat-topped brothers. That gave me the opportunity to try and shake some consciousness back into my head and attempt to get back on my feet. It was hard to make out what was going on but I could see that Vince was back on his feet. It seemed like over a dozen guys were throwing punches at each other and they were all connecting. No one was attempting to dodge, weave or intercept the oncoming blows and knuckles were flying everywhere.

Knocker obviously got bored of this and took a run straight into the centre of the melee with his arms outstretched. He hit two guys at about throat height and one of them fell backwards against the urinals and cracked his head as he fell. As his face almost landed in the piss-filled gutter I could see blood seeping from his head wound onto those little yellow cubes that lie amongst the fag-ends and spittle near the drain. The other guy that had been clothes-lined was made of sterner stuff and he gripped Knocker in something resembling a head lock and began bashing his quiffed-up head against the hand-dryers. As I began to launch myself back into the fray I got a jarring blow to the head and as I stepped back in shock I found that the guy I had kicked into the cubicle was back in action with obviously only me in his sights. As he continued to throw punches I managed to grab his curly-permed hair tightly and I tried as hard as I could to bring his face down onto my knee. I could not make contact as hard as I would have liked but it burst his nose with alarming ease and as he broke free and raised his head, he sent an arc of blood splashing against my T-shirt. Once again he staggered back into the cubicle but this time he was out much quicker and from his trouser pocket he had pulled out a particularly rusty-looking Stanley knife.

  Despite the adrenalin rush I was experiencing I also felt a real flash of fear as getting scarred for life had not really been at the forefront of my mind as I had carefully prepared my quiff earlier in the evening. I took a few steps back in a bit of a blind panic and tried to kick out as his knife-wielding hand. He saw the kicks coming a long way off and started jabbing at me with the blade. The first lunge hit the toe of my boot but after a few more plunges he made contact and stabbed the knife into my shin. The pain was sharp and intense but the sight of my blood making a growing stain on my trouser leg filled me more with rage than agony. Bernie was wrestling with one of the Slough mob and managed to land something midway between a shove and a judo throw on his opponent which jarred against the geezer who cut me. The knife dropped from his hand and the dozy bastard bent down to retrieve his blood-stained blade giving me a stone cold opportunity to lay my boot right on his face. Once again he was on his back in the same cubicle but he looked as if he had little intention of getting up. Despite the fact that it would have been a good time to help out my mates, I was fucking furious and I moved towards the cubicle. The guy was still stunned and half collapsed on the floor but I noticed that his hand was resting on the toilet seat. I forced the toilet lid down onto his fingers then stomped hard on it. He soon broke out of his stupor and screamed loudly. I stamped again on the seat and as his yells increased a few of his mates obviously realised what was going on and made a lunge for me.

At this point, the pub's bouncers joined us in the gents, having taken the time to arm themselves with an array of bats, coshes and pool cues. We all knew that these geezers were amongst Stevenage's most hardened, full-time thugs and (perhaps subconsciously) we all took a step or two back and let our enemies take the first wave of punishment. We were not to escape unscathed though and we all got some form of whacking as we were dragged through the pub and dumped in the street. Before we could even regroup and swap war stories there was a yell from across the street and another twenty or so punters, who were obviously attached to the guys we had been scrapping with, made a charge in our direction. They had obviously been in some other boozer and word had reached them about the battle in The Coach. As we had already had a fair beating there was no real room for heroics and we all had it off on our toes. As they obviously had no real understanding of New Town street planning, we melted like ghosts into the maze of underpasses and walkways that lead to the town centre and they soon gave up the chase. The dozy bastards then launched into some moronic chant which eventually faded into the distance. We walked on to just behind St George's Church where we took a breather to compare war wounds. My leg was still bleeding but it did not look too serious and Knocker had a small cut above his eye, probably from his head-on collision with a hand-dryer.

Bernie was looking at my leg and doom-mongering, 'You'd better get that checked Harry. You could get aids.'

'You don't get aids from a fucking Stanley knife,' I told him.

'Yeh,' said Stevie, 'You're more likely to get it off a bog seat in the Coach.'

We started to laugh a bit, more from the adrenalin buzz than Stevie's great joke then Bernie and Knocker began to get a bit more agitated.

'We've got to go back,' said Bernie, 'We've got to finish this.'

'Yeh,' said Knocker as he shouted to no one in particular, 'Give me 10p!'

'What for?' I said as he waved an outstretched palm in front of us all.

'Just give me 10p,' he growled. 'I'm going to phone Shane and Kev and anyone else who wants to give these bastards some back.'

I was not particularly keen on a revenge attack but most of the guys looked well up for it so I kept my mouth shut.

Almost an hour later we were still behind St. George's and I was starting to get pissed off. Someone had been dispatched to the local off-licence and we were downing a few cans of Special Brew but the buzz from the fight had more or less faded for me and all I felt was a dull ache in my leg wound and a general all-over stiffness. Knocker and Bernie were still trying to whip up a war party but a few of the guys were starting to lose a little enthusiasm for a further ruck with the Slough casuals. There was a low rumbling sound down the street and it was growing louder. Soon Kenny Priest's ancient van rolled around the corner and the side door slid open with a screech to reveal Shane, Kev and a few other bodies.

'Get in,' shouted Kenny.

We drained what was left in our cans, threw them to the ground and piled into the van. The pain in my leg was starting to fade.

Along with Shane, Kev and a variety of bats, chains and clubs, Kenny had recruited three of his old Punk mates and a local Ted called Crazy Steve, an ageing Scotsman who was built like Mick McManus. They were all battle ready Stevenage boys who had been treading their own path, and occasionally treading on each other, long before most of us had our first flat-tops. Neither of them were particularly talkative and only seemed to be here for the aggro rather than any great desire to help us out. Kenny was pretty quiet too, just driving slowly and looking for his target.

'Is that them?' he piped up and Knocker leant over the front seat to take a look.

'Oh yes,' he said, almost licking his lips.

Kenny pulled over but kept the van running. I took a peek out the side vent of the van and saw about twenty of the Slough geezers across the road queuing outside The Long Ship nightclub. They appeared to have pushed their way to the front, judging by the pissed-off faces of the punters behind them, and were arguing the toss with the bouncers who appeared to be undecided over whether to take their money or turn them away.

One of the Punks stood up in the van and grabbed what looked like a particularly heavy sink plunger, 'Let's fucking do them!'

'Hold on, hold on,' said Kev in a hushed tone then he leaned casually out of the passenger side window. His silent staring and sharp blonde quiff soon attracted the attention of one of the crowd who broke off from haranguing the doormen and sauntered across to the van with a drunken swagger.

'Hey! Billy Idol,' he shouted as he crossed the road, 'We had a few of your mates tonight.'

'What mate?' said Kev innocently, reeling in the unsuspecting nitwit like a dozy pike.

'I said we kicked the shit out of a bunch of freaks like you,' slurred the geezer as he almost leant in the window.

As soon as he was close enough, Kev grabbed the back of the guy's head and pulled his face furiously against the van door.

As Kev's victim dropped to the ground Kenny screamed, 'Let's do it!', and leapt from the van with a bike chain in his grip.

The side door was pulled open and we all piled out. Kenny's scream had alerted the Slough mob who turned away from pestering the bouncers but stood rooted to the pavement. The doormen quickly ducked into the club, slamming the doors behind them, and any unsuspecting club goers in the queue melted away to a safe viewing position.

As I left the van I realised that I had not grabbed a weapon of any kind and I frantically reached back into the transit for something. The first thing I could lay my hands on was a thermos flask and, as I cursed my luck, I thought I might as well put it to some use and threw it over the heads of my rapidly advancing mates. I had never been any good at school sports but by some sheer stroke of luck it sailed straight into the middle of the Slough boys and hit one of the cunts right above the eye. My second foray across the van floor landed me with what looked like somebody's little sister's hockey stick and, assuming it was the best I would get, I joined the fight.

Although the Slough boys stood their ground, with a few reaching for their Stanleys, our tooled-up mob descended on them like locusts and their backs were against the wall under a rain of blows. Crazy Steve and the Punks had not seemed to have enjoyed a rumble for sometime and appeared particularly keen to crack as many heads as possible. One of the Punks even broke away from us, having beaten a couple of guys to the ground, and launched his crowbar into a nearby Dixon's window adding the shrill ring of the shop's alarm to the general melee. Even before I got to the outside of the club most of the Slough mob were either down on the pavement or heading that way so I concentrated on hitting anyone who looked in danger of getting up. Kenny Priest was thrashing away with his bike chain with such abandon that he caught Vince across the head with it as he took another swing, and all around was the sound of boots pounding against pastel-coloured clobber.

Our Punk mate's one man wave of anarchy against the retail trade had attracted the local plod far quicker than the ruckus and as we heard the squeal of approaching sirens we started to move back to the van. As we bundled into the transit, once again I was at the back and I noticed yet more of the Slough boys approaching from further up the road.

'C'mon,' I shouted. 'Get going. There is fucking more of them!'

The bastards must have colonised the town by the bus load. Where were they all coming from? Before I could get in the van I looked up once again to judge how close they were. Just in time to see a glistening shape sail through the air and feel it smash against my forehead. I saw a brief flash of coloured lights and felt something warm run down my face then… nothing. Goodnight.

# Chapter 6
## Sex Beat Crazy

I was lying in bed giving my dick a bit of a squeeze but undecided over whether to attempt a full-blown wank when Vince and Knocker burst into the room.

'Wakey, wakey, hand's off snakey,' yelled Vince and threw a crumpled brown paper bag on the bed.

'What's this?' I said as I opened the crumpled package. All it contained was a can of Breaker.

'Get well soon, eh!' said Knocker as he walked over to my record collection.

I placed the can on my bedside table and struggled to pull myself up to a seated position.

'How you been?' asked Vince as he flopped down onto the bottom of my bed.

'My fucking head still hurts,' I said and winced a bit for effect.

The old wincing, sighing and groaning had been working a treat on my mum and dad, and resulted in all sorts of pampering but Vince barely acknowledged it.

'You coming out on Friday? Frenzy are playing at the Headstone,' piped up Knocker.

'I can't go out yet,' I whined, 'I look like fucking Frankenstein.'

Our fracas with the Slough boys had resulted in an A&E visit for me after I was hit on the forehead with a bottle. It could probably have been worse, as I dropped like a stone, but the guys managed to bundle me into the van before the howling mob descended. Kenny drove me straight to Lister hospital where the night staff had little patience for another 'hooligan' casualty and battered thirteen stitches into my bonce with no anaesthetic.

To make matters worse, the old bill made a visit to the hospital and hit me with some type of disturbing the peace charge. I was furious at the injustice. Some fucking poser numbskulls take a Stanley knife and a beer bottle to me but the police can not see beyond my partly shaved head and boots and suddenly I am the villain. Okay, so we left about ten of them battered and bleeding outside a nightclub but surely we were the innocent party?

'Oh, let's have some of this.' Knocker pulled a Torment album from it's sleeve and slapped it down on my turntable.

'Woah!' I moaned, 'Take it easy with that.' I treated all my vinyl with respect but Knocker was not particular, especially the way he stabbed the needle onto the record and fumbled roughly with the volume knob as if it was some bird's sweaty nipple.

'You've got to come to the gig Harry. It's Knocker's going away bash,' said Vince.

'Why? Where are you going? Rampton?' I quipped.

'No,' said Knocker flatly, 'My uncle's got me a job on the steel erecting in Germany. That's not all I'll be erecting either.'

'You fancy your chances there?'

'Too fucking right. Those German birds, they're far more open-minded. I read about it in Fiesta, they get up to all sorts.'

Vince giggled, 'He'll be popping it in everywhere. The dirty bastard.'

'You're not wrong there mate,' smirked Knocker, 'You know me. As long as there is a little heat in there somewhere.'

Why Knocker had as much success with the ladies as he did always amazed me. His patter was lousy and the way he treated his string of girlfriends and one night stands was a long way from the age of chivalry. Nonetheless, he simply believed that he could pull the birds and his stonewall confidence more often than not got results. If he did not succeed he merely shrugged it off and moved on. If I ever got a knock-back it crushed me, at least until I was on the piss again.

'So when are you leaving?' I asked.

'Two weeks,' said Knocker as he dragged the needle abruptly off the vinyl and onto the next track.

'You really fancy it then?' said Vince.

'Why not? There is fuck all happening round here and its good money.'

Vince was already starting to get bored of the visit and started eying the can of Breaker on my bedside cabinet, 'Are you going to drink that?'

'Not tonight.'

'Give us a sip then,' he said reaching over.

'What?' I said loudly, 'I thought it was a get well gift?'

'Crack it open you tight bastard,' said Knocker.

Vince took a deep draught from the can and passed it to Knocker. By the time it reached me, there was little more than floaters in the can. I gulped it down anyway.

In a way, Knocker's leaving party kick-started my recovery. Once I had decided to go I knew that I would have to get back to work, just in case some grass from the factory spotted me out on the piss and stuck the boot in with my employers. Why I was worried about offending Thatcher's slave trading scheme was a bit of a mystery but I enjoyed working with Bernie and simply did not want to let him down.

When I returned to work on Monday my stitched forehead looked pretty raw and my eyes were still puffy and black. Luckily, making road signs does not particularly require any form of male modelling. During the week I managed to catch up with a few of the guys even though, apart from Knocker and Vince, none of the bastards made any attempt to visit me while I was banged up in bed. When Friday came around I was feeling a lot better and more than ready for a booze up and, if possible, a bunk-up so I spent a bit more time than usual with my quiff in the hope it would attract the ladies' attention away from my battered boat race.

I was glad that I had forced myself out of bed for Knocker's leaving party and it was good to be back out again after too many nights scratching my nuts at home. Kenny took us all down to Harrow in his trusty transit and the atmosphere at the Headstone was excellent with Frenzy playing on top form yet again. I was starting to tire a bit though as the gig was drawing to a close until Knocker strolled out of the crowd and grabbed me by the arm.

'Harry, you've got to come with me mate.'

'Why? What's happening?'

'I've got a bird over there. She's well up for it but she don't want to leave her mate behind. I told her you would come back with us and keep her friend occupied.'

'Oh, for fuck's sake.' I said. 'Have you set me up to babysit some boiler while you fuck her mate? No way, forget it.'

'Oh come on,' replied Knocker, 'It's my last night.'

'What? And that's the reason why I should spend the night with some bird I don't even know?'

'Listen,' he said quietly, 'You'll get a shag out of it.'

'How do you know?' I sighed.

'Cos I've asked her. I pointed you out to her and she's up for it.'

'You've got to be joking?' I said in shock.

'No. Look it's that skinny Goth girl over there. Next to the big rock chick with the massive tits. She's mine.'

'Oh, I get it. You get Bonnie Tyler and I get Olive Oyl.'

'She's not bad,' said Knocker. 'Anyway, it's the best you'll get over the next few weeks. You said it yourself, you look like fucking scarface.'

'Cheers,' I said, but he did have a point and it had been some time since I had last had a leg-over.

I reluctantly agreed to Knocker's seedy plan and as the gig drew to a close we parted company with the rest of the crew who were heading back to Stevenage.

'You're fucking mad Powell,' said Vince, 'She's a right dog. Don't think much of Knocker's either. He's not fussy. He'd shag a hole in a fur coat.'

'Owt's better than nowt mate,' I replied. 'She's not that bad.'

The truth was, I had warmed to the situation and with my beer goggles on the girl looked quite cute and her tight, black rubber dress and knee-high boots were already giving my John Thomas a twinge. Her name was Anita and Knocker's new friend was called Michelle. In the taxi back to Michelle's house, as Knocker and his latest conquest got down to some heavy petting, I attempted to strike up some conversation.

'So where is the party then?' I asked.

'We're going back to Michelle's,' was all she said then went mute again.

After an awkward silence I realised that it was up to me to get some banter flowing but it was fucking hard work. Most of my chat was met with one-word answers and all I could find out was that she was indeed called Anita, she worked for the council and she generally found life in Harrow 'boring'. Attempting to chat this girl up was so painful that I was almost thinking of doing a runner as the taxi stopped but I decided to persevere as, with Kenny and the crew probably shooting up the A1, I was stranded for the night anyway.

Knocker and Michelle were all over each other as we made our way into a terraced house in the middle of god knows where. Almost as soon as we were through the front Anita grabbed my hand and led me upstairs.

'We're up here, c'mon.'

I was a bit shocked as that was probably the most she had said all night. She dragged me into a bedroom and switched on a tiny bedside lamp which gave the room a faint orange glow.

'Shut the door then,' she ordered as she sat on the bed and began unfastening her kinky boots.

I obliged and as I turned to face her once again she kicked off the boots, stood up and deftly pulled her dress off over her head with one swift move. She stood close to me wearing only a tiny pair of black pants, stockings and suspenders and revealing her small but pert breasts.

'Are you ready?' she said.

At first I was a bit shocked at the pace of this mating ritual but my bell-end soon got the message and I took her in my arms and launched into some tongue lashing. As I stroked her back and slid my hands onto her bare arse cheeks she began tugging on my zip and belt buckle in a bid to free my stiffening member. We sat on the bed for a moment as I got my boots off and all the while she was running her hands across my chest and occasionally stroking my cock. As soon as I was stripped as nature intended I lay down with her on the bed and began the removal of her knickers. The little minx had them worn over her suspenders so they slid off easily leaving her silky stockings on but her moist muff open and ready for a poking. I rubbed her warm opening with my fingers and, as we continued to kiss passionately, her hands were stroking me all over and her body was writhing frantically beneath me. I could barely believe this was the same girl who had appeared to have the personality of a waxwork earlier on. Suddenly she broke off from her ecstatic wriggling and held my face in her hands.

She stared deeply into my eyes and whispered, 'Do you want to play a game?'

I was initially a bit shocked and hoped that a game of naked Monopoly was not what she had in mind.

'What?... do you mean... will we...'

'Don't panic,' she giggled, 'It's a sex game.'

'Oh, alright,' I mumbled, still confused as to where this was leading.

She laughed a little bit and clapped her hands excitedly like a kid on Christmas morning. Then she broke away from me and leant over the other side of the bed to get something. I decided right then that if it was a twelve-inch dildo with my name on it then I was off. With a mixture of relief and surprise I saw her pull a small bongo drum from a tatty Woolworth's carrier bag. Anita lay back down close to me and laid the drum beside her at arm's length. She bit her lip gently, heaved her breasts a little and opened her legs wide.

'Can you keep the beat Harry?'

What happened next was certainly one of the most unusual ways I have spent a Friday night. The theme of the game was that I would get on top of her in a traditional missionary position but time my thrusts inside her to the beat that she banged out on the drum. Her drumming took a pretty even pace to start with but then she began to speed up for short bursts then slow down for long periods. I tried my best to keep my pumping rhythmic but her fast / slow combinations almost had me at the vinegar strokes a few times. Mainly because I was attempting to concentrate on her erratic drum beats, I did manage to keep it going for a while and Anita began to groan climactically. I kissed her fully on the lips then stared straight into her eyes.

'Bang that fucking thing,' I said and gestured to the bongo.

'Keep the beat Harry,' she panted and started to bash the drum like Keith Moon in full flow.

I had no trouble matching that rhythm.

After our sex bout Anita almost reverted back to the catatonic state she had been in the taxi. Eventually I managed to get some conversation out of her then wished I had not. She launched into a lengthy diatribe about how bad her life was, stuck in a boring job in a boring town but seemingly unwilling to do anything about it. As I lay there listening to her painfully slow droning on there was some sort of disturbance downstairs. I could hear raised voices and a door being banged furiously. I was actually quite glad of the interruption as it gave me the perfect excuse to get out of bed and pull my clobber back on. I tied my boots loosely and threw on my jeans and T-shirt.

'What's going on?' said Anita, as if it had only dawned on her that something was wrong.

'It's kicking off downstairs,' I said as I peeked out the bedroom window. 'What the fuck is going on?'

'It's probably just Mike, back from the rugby club,' she sighed.

Outside on the street was a mini-bus full of about ten pug-nosed bruisers. They had obviously heard the commotion and they were starting to spill out onto the street to investigate.

'Who the fuck is Mike?' I said but did not wait for an answer as Anita looked as if offering an explanation would tire her out.

At the bottom of the stairs Knocker seemed to have pulled on his gear and was arguing with a fairly big lump of a bloke wearing the standard rugby player uniform of dress shirt, jeans and brown leather brogues. Michelle was in the background wrapped only in a sleeping bag and weeping.

'Mike… I don't know what to say. It just

happened.'

'Shut your mouth you strumpet. I don't fucking believe this,' he yelled back.

'Hold up, hold up,' said Knocker quite calmly, 'I know this is your sister but she is a big girl. She can take care of herself.'

'My sister?' screamed Mike.

'Well that's what she told me.'

'That's my wife you fucking freak!'

The 'freak' bit may have been a bit too much for Knocker, or maybe he was just bored with the domestic, but either way he stuck the nut on the geezer sending him crashing onto a small telephone table.

'Knocker,' I yelled as I clattered down the stairs. 'Shut that fucking door.'

No sooner had Knocker slammed the door than angry fists began thumping on it from outside. Mike had also emerged quickly from Knocker's stunning blow and had his fists flaying in our direction. After a brief tussle which turned the rest of the hall furniture to matchwood we managed to get him down again and laid into him with our boots in an attempt to get him off our backs. Even then Mike kept coming while Michelle shrieked in alarm and his mates continued to pound on the door. He had a firm grip on Knocker and was dragging him to the floor while at the same time the door was creaking from the increasing punishment it was receiving from the baying mob outside. I started to panic and looked for some way to bring the confrontation to a close. My solution was to pick up the telephone that was lying on the floor and repeatedly whack Mike over the head with it until he loosened his grip on Knocker. As we fled out the back door the front door was popping off its hinges followed by a gang of thick-necked vengeance seekers. We leapt over the garden fence like Olympians and ran blindly down the street.

So that was how I spent Knocker's last night in

the UK; a cold, empty shag followed by an hour or so of being chased like a dog across Harrow by a gang of thugs. They eventually gave up and Knocker and I spent the rest of the evening lying on benches near a bus stop. Still, at least Frenzy had been good and as far as cold, empty shags go it had not really been that bad.

# Chapter 7
# Squeeze Play

In the two months following Knocker's departure things were very quiet. Surely he was not the glue that held the entire British Psychobilly scene together? The rest of us did nothing much else but booze it up at each other's houses or shuffle between the local ale houses at the weekend. Co-incidentally, I did notice a few regulars at the Bowes Lyon, who lived out of town, had ditched their Psychobilly style in favour of a more Gothic look. Clad in all-black clobber, with Cramps or Sunglasses After Dark T-shirts and growing their hair longer, it looked as if they were slowly distancing themselves from the scene. A few others were less subtle and now sported a full Smiths-inspired look of floppy quiffs, beads and junk shop suits. While I am all for a 'live and let live' policy regarding folk's particular musical tastes, I found it odd that they could desert the Psychobilly lifestyle so rapidly. For me, Psychobilly was everything and without it I would have no mates, no interests and only my mum, dad and sister's nagging to keep me company. Each to his own I suppose… the bandwagon-jumping, fashion-casualty, turncoat fuckwits!

As Winter approached, things seemed to be rolling again and one night, after a hard day's sign making, I returned home to find a scribbled note with my name on it lying on the kitchen table.

'What's this?' I shouted into the living room.

'Some bloke phoned,' my dad shouted back, 'Vance, I think it was. He said to give you that message.'

I opened the crumpled sheet and peered at my dad's scrawl - Coffin Nails. Reading Majestic. This Friday night. Pick you at 7. Kenny's van.

'Did he say anything else?' I yelled.

'Yes, he said "thanks grandad" to me. The cheeky bastard.'

I giggled and strode upstairs to my room, making a move directly towards my stereo. This was good news, another gig at last. I pulled the 'Zorch Factor One' album from my collection. I could feel the buzz starting already.

As Friday night came around, Kenny was bang on. He was parping his horn furiously at 7pm but I was ready. Quiff done, boots polished and three cans of Breaker down my neck I was out the door almost immediately. I threw my pilot jacket and another four cans of beer onto the skanky floor of Kenny's van and jumped in. Kenny, Shona and Lynne were upfront and Stan, Vince, Stevie, Shane, Kev and Baz were huddled together in the back.

'Powell, you old poof,' someone shouted just before Kenny pulled the oldest trick in the book and jerked the van forward sharply before I had a chance to sit down. I was sent sprawling onto the mass of bodies, beer cans and burning fag ends. Everyone cheered. We were off.

We had all seen The Coffin Nails before at the Klub Foot so we knew we were in for a good time. It was a hometown gig for them and the place was packed. We all wandered around the venue chatting to some punters that we knew from other towns and had met at gigs before in between bouts of queuing at the bar. After the drought of the last few months it was great to be back at another Psychobilly gig. Despite this we still did not see much of the support band. Later on, the odd tuning-up twang could be heard and The Coffin Nails took to the stage. The air crackled with excitement, the band started and everyone in the hall moved that bit closer to the dancefloor. Within minutes a wrecking pit had started and I dived in. After over eight weeks of inaction it is amazing how much I had missed being beaten senseless in front of a live band.

Throughout the band's set the wrecking was fucking fierce. Most of the night, all manner of fists and elbows were working me over but the buzz from the music, along with eight cans of breaker and a couple of lines of cheap speed, dulled the pain. By the time they had finished though I was knackered and I felt that the heat of the venue combined with a general fug of spilt beer, fags and sweaty bodies was overwhelming. I made my way outside, making sure that the bouncers clocked me so that I could get back in. Within seconds the cold night air attached itself to my sweaty torso so I put on the T-shirt which I had jammed into the waistband of my jeans. The shirt was also soaked in sweat, probably from other punters, and I did not feel much warmer. It was good to get a breath of fresh air again. So good that I lit up another roll-up.

There were a few other punters from the club scattered around the car park in small groups. I did not particularly recognise any of them but I noticed a very good looking Psychobilly girl sitting on a small wall. Flushed with the excitement of the gig and, for a change, not yet incapacitated with the booze I thought I would give her some chat. I had nothing to lose but a knock back and maybe it was time I used some of Knocker's brutish charm. As I got closer I almost bottled it a bit as I realised that she was beyond very good looking and banging on the door marked gorgeous. Her quiff was jet black, sharp and immaculate with a thick strip of hair hanging down in front of each ear just like the skinhead birds sported. The back and sides of her head were shaved to a number one and she had a smooth, pale complexion highlighted starkly with her bright red lipstick. Her figure was not too shabby either and she was wearing only tight black jeans and a black vest under her olive pilot jacket. I could easily see that none of her curves were out of place and her zebra-striped creepers were the final touch of class. I took a deep breath, launched my fag end into the gutter and launched my charm offensive.

'Is anyone sitting here?' I said pointing at the wall and immediately realised the shite start I had made in my chat-up attempt.

'Does it look like it?' she said with mild annoyance.

I forged ahead blindly and sat down next to her, 'Have you been to gigs here before?'

'What? Do you mean do I come here often?' she said sarcastically.

I paused for a moment then stood up and began to move back to the venue, 'Look, sorry. Fuck it. This chat-up is poor,' I admitted.

'Is that what you were trying to do? Chat me up?' she smiled and looked even more beautiful.

'Well, y'now. I thought it was worth a bash.'

'Worth a bash?' she laughed, 'You cheeky bastard.'

I could see that she was giving me a good-natured wind-up, then she thrust one of her roll-ups towards me as a peace offering. I sat back down and pulled out my trusty zippo. A gentle breeze was blowing so she lent forward and cupped her hands around mine as she lit her cigarette. There was another moment of contact as she drew back and her quiff gently brushed across my face. Even that slight motion gave my percy a twinge of anticipation.

'The pace too much for you then?' she said.

'You're not joking,' I replied, 'It's a fucking war zone in there. The locals don't half like having a pop at the visitors.'

'I wouldn't worry about it. When there is no-one else here they beat each other up just as much.'

'Are you a Reading girl then?' I asked.

'Not far from here, just up at Henley. What about you?'

'Stevenage.'

She smirked, 'The concrete jungle, eh? You all right crossing the road love?'

'Just about. It's not all underpasses you know.'

'I'm only taking the piss,' she laughed and nudged my leg with hers, giving my John Thomas another jolt in the progress.

'So are you waiting out here for someone?' I asked.

She paused for a moment, blew a sharp puff of smoke through her pursed lips then turned to me and smiled.

'Look, before you start going round the houses, I'm here with a few mates and I haven't got a boyfriend.'

I let out a deep breath, 'Fair enough,' then after a short pause, 'I'm Harry by the way.'

'How nice to meet you Harry,' she said with mock politeness, 'I'm Clau.'

'Clow?' I questioned a bit more loudly than I had intended.

'Yeh Clau. My mum and dad call me Claudia.'

'Oh right. I see.' I stood up and held out my arm with the exaggerated gesture of a Victorian dandy, 'Shall we return to the ball Claudia?'

She got the joke and gave me a flash of her pearly whites.

'Why yes kind sir,' she said as she gripped onto my arm.

A few of the guys clocked me returning to the dancehall with Claudia and they gave me a bit of breathing space to continue my chat. As soon as she went to the bog though Vince, Barry and Stan were over in a shot.

'What were you up to outside with her?' said

Vince.

    'Just chatting.'
    Barry was having none of it.
    'Fuck off, what's been going on?'
    'Nothing,' I replied, 'Just some chat.'
    'You fucking poof. You should have been poking her at least, she's a tidy piece,' said Stan in one of his many bursts of subtlety.
    'You mind your own fucking business,' I told him. 'There will be poking when I'm ready to poke.'

Getting to know Claudia was far more prominent in my mind but Stan's witless statement brought out my macho bravado in some stupid way. You see amongst my mates, steady girlfriends were something of a threat and relationships were often only thought of as things that would get in the way of what you wanted to do - which was basically piss about, drink booze and listen to Psychobilly. In reality, most of these problems came about amongst the guys who had straight girlfriends, girls who were not interested in any aspect of the Psychobilly scene or any underground movement. These partners were often old sweethearts from our school days or the odd trendy bird from the neighbourhood. To these girls, the Psychobilly scene only ever represented an inconvenience or annoyance, such as gigs which dragged their boyfriend away every other weekend and left them at home twiddling their thumbs. Relationships of this kind could only end in two ways; with the romance crashing to an abrupt end or, the unthinkable, with the guy being dragged away from his mates and leaving the Psychobilly lifestyle behind.

    Kenny and Stan's girlfriends were a different breed though. Shona and Lynne were hard-core Psychobillies themselves and for them they were around for the music and lifestyle more than anything. Before discovering Psychobilly they had both been rude girls during the Two-Tone boom. Despite how much a part of the crew the girls were, on the odd occasions that they were not around Stan and Kenny more often than not would be sniffing like hogs around any girl within a half-mile radius. It would not be me in their position, Lynne and Shona were a right couple of knuckle girls who were unafraid to dish out a slap to anyone. I always suspected that if Kenny and Stan ever got caught playing away they would find their nuts crushed between a couple of house bricks. So far though I had little experience in locking lips with a true Psychobilly woman but maybe things were about to change.

'So who is poking who?' said Claudia as she suddenly appeared at my side having obviously heard my idle boast.

I immediately got flustered, a sure sign of guilt, and tried to move the conversation in another direction.

'Clau, these are Barry, Vince and Stan. Three tramps I found living in a Stevenage underpass. Guys this is Clau.'

'Alright love,' said Stan in a sleazy manner while clocking an eyeful of her ample bosom.

Vince and Barry also said their hello's but not much else as the volume in the club was still pretty loud and, even though the band were long gone, the DJ was still spinning a selection of Psychobilly and Rockabilly favourites with some Goth tracks thrown in to keep the local pale-faces happy. Surprisingly the guys said their goodbyes and moved away to give me a bit of space. As they walked towards the bar, it struck me that Vince and Baz looked particularly deep in conversation.

Claudia and I got on pretty well throughout the rest of the evening but she was not too heavy and I went back to my mates a few times, despite the fact that all they were interested in was whether I had secured a promise of a shag for the night. I noticed that she was pretty popular amongst the locals and chatted to a lot of guys but she always ended up back with me and eventually we got to grips in a small corridor near the bogs. I held her tight and we got into a liplock with some light tongue work. My hands were soon on her butt cheeks and as I squeezed her against the wall she pushed her arse back against the brickwork making my bum gripping even firmer. Her hands stroked the back of my head and neck and I could feel her shapely knockers pressed against me. I was sure she could feel my caged hard-on as it strained to break through the two layers of denim and undies which held us apart. I started gently grinding against her in a manner that gave any one passing by a clear illustration of my intentions.

'Easy tiger!' she said, breaking off from our clinch, 'You'll get me done for public indecency.'

I smiled but said nothing and got back to the kissing. I did take note though and made an attempt to calm down my dry-running. At least until later.

'How did you get on with that bird tonight?' asked Vince through a cloud of hash smoke.

I was perched on the wheel arch of Kenny's van and attempting to keep my balance while rolling another three-skinner.

'Fine mate. Fine,' I said and gave no more away.

'What he means is, did you fuck her?' piped up Stan from the front seats.

'Shut your mouth you dirty bastard,' said Shona and punched him in the ribs.

'I was only asking my sweet darling,' said Stan, continuing to take the piss while planting a few slobbering kisses on her.

'Well, what did you get?' continued Vince.

'Yeh, let's hear it,' added Baz, 'Don't hold back. I'm planning on a wank later.'

'I got plenty you nosy bastards, that is all you

need to know.'

Vince shrugged his shoulders and clapped his hands together, 'Oh, no. That's it, he's in love again.'

'Fuck off! No I'm not.'

'Oh yes, it's the same every time. If you get a grip on some sort that you are never going to see again we get a stroke by stroke commentary. If it's a bird you are serious about you go all coy,' sneered Vince.

'Bollocks,' was all I could come up with.

The truth was, Vince was right. Before Kenny started peeping the van's horn and threatening to let me walk back to Stevenage, Claudia and I had been up an alley at the side of the Majestic indulging in some pretty heavy petting. I certainly got the impression that she may have been easily persuaded to take it further but it was actually me who held back. There must be some puritan streak in my ancestry but I feel that I do not want to see any girl again that drops the drawers on the first night. I am quite happy to oblige any girl that dishes out everything immediately but I will not be phoning them back during the week. I would certainly even bunk them up again if our paths crossed on a night out but even then I would not be pestering them for a date. Why bother when I have already had a taste of their goodies. I was pretty sure that I would be seeing Claudia again, I had her number, so I had held back even though my dick was petitioning for a first night fuck. It was a gamble, until I phoned her I had no idea whether I could guarantee a future knee-trembler but I felt it was a safe bet.

The guys did not get any more out of me and after about a quarter of an hour of persisting they gave up. Inside the van we all sort of drifted into a stoned silence. As we sped past the 'Welcome To Stevenage New Town' road sign, cracks of daylight were starting to appear in the night sky. I was one of the last to be deposited from the back of the van and as I dusted myself off I bid goodnight to Kenny and Lynne. Kenny waved wearily but obviously he still had enough energy to pop a wheel spin as he screeched out of my street. The sun was rising slowly and the place was bathed in that peculiar blue light that only postmen, insomniacs and all-night drinkers get to appreciate. I sat on the low wall next to the block of garages which faced our house and relit the dog end of a joint which had been crushed in my jacket pocket. After a few tokes I hit the cork and blew out that final acrid puff that lurks at the end of every doobie.

       Seeing The Coffin Nails play would have been more than enough to make it a great night but meeting Claudia had been extra special. I made a brief, startled lunge into my pockets to ensure I still had her number then parped out a little sigh of relief as I found the precious notepaper crunched into a ball amongst my loose change. I thought about how cool she had been, especially after my initial bungled chat-up line and I also remembered those great knockers pressed against me and how firm her butt cheeks had felt. With this in mind I was awoken from my dozing state and I made a determined move to get into the house. There was wanking to be done.

# Chapter 8
# The Spirit of 69

'Claudia? Its me,' I said down the phone.

'Mr Powell. How nice of you to call… at last. I thought I had been given the bum's rush,' said Claudia.

'Are you joking? I just thought I would try to find a gap in your social calendar.'

She laughed and I grinned to myself. That was a nice bit of bullshit. The truth was I had not phoned her through a combination of wondering if she would still be interested and not wanting to phone her too soon and seem desperate. I also wanted to have a bit of peace and quiet to lay on some charm without my family ear-wigging on my conversation. Wednesday was the only night I could get the gaff to myself.

'So what have you been up to?' I asked.

'Nothing much,' she replied. 'I don't really go out much during the week. I see my mate Carla sometimes. Occasionally there is an Indie band on at the Majestic on Thursday nights. Nothing special.'

'That's a good venue,' I said. 'That Coffin Nails gig was excellent. Good atmosphere. I got a nice set of bruises.'

She giggled, 'Yeh, the guys down there get a bit wild but they are all right. They didn't make you too unwelcome did they?'

'Only cause I was with you I reckon.'

'Aw,' she taunted, 'Did I protect you Harry?'

'You certainly gave me the kiss of life.'

'Well,' purred Claudia, 'You might get some resuscitation next time I see you.'

Ding dong! There it was. I waved my fist silently in the air. An action replay was definitely on. I had to play it cool though. I had blown it in the past with some real tasty sorts by being too eager.

'I like the sound of that. So any gigs on this weekend?' Whoops, bit of a clumsy change of subject there. 'Don't fuck it up,' I thought to myself.

'Eh… no… nothing this weekend. I think Restless are playing in December', she said.

There was a bit of an awkward pause and I bottled it a bit. Fuck it! It was eager or nothing.

'Listen Claudia, I'd really like to see you again some time. Do you fancy it?'

Her voice seemed to brighten immediately, 'That would be great Harry. How about this weekend?'

'Brilliant. I can get a loan of my dad's car and take you out. You don't mind being seen in a Vauxhall Viva do you?'

'I've got a better idea. My folks are away on Saturday, why don't you come down and we could have a night in?'

I felt an immediate stiffening in my trousers, agreed enthusiastically and took down her address.

'Fantastic. Saturday night it is the Miss… eh. What is your second name anyway?'

'Quigley,' she said in mock shock, 'I told you last week you drunken bum. Do you even remember what I look like?'

'I won't forget that in a hurry,' I replied.

'You fucking smoothy,' she laughed, 'Get back to your Bryan Ferry records.'

We said our goodbyes and I hung up the phone. I felt a bit lightheaded and moved into the garden for a breath of fresh air. It was dark outside but there are so many streetlights in Stevenage that the place is constantly bathed in an orange glow. There was a warm, pleasant buzz in my stomach and also a sense of relief that the phone call had went so well. I had not really been that bothered about scoring a follow-up date with any of the girls which I had locked lips with in the past few years. It always seemed too much effort going out with someone who I had simply fell on top of at closing time the week before. With most of them, all we had in common was that we were both drunk and randy in the same place at the same time. I had hoped Claudia would be different but it looked as if another grunt and grapple session was on the cards at least. I did hope it would lead to more though. I pursed my lips together in practice. I was going to have to kiss my dad's arse if I wanted to borrow his bleedin' car.

I had intended to keep my date with Claudia under wraps, at least until I had seen how it went, but I have always been a bad liar and when Vince and Baz came over to my house the following night they soon got the truth out of me.

'Don't give me all that pony. Staying in?' shouted Baz, 'You must be seeing that bird you copped off with at the Majestic. Am I right?'

I admitted defeat, I just do not have that poker face.

'Well why didn't you just say that?'

'Yeh,' added Vince, 'What's the big deal? You are just going to get a shag, aren't you?'

'Yeh, I know, but…,' I stuttered.

'Hold up, hold up,' said Baz, 'You're not serious about her are you? What do you want a full-time bird for? We always get plenty spare, don't we?'

I felt as if I was being hauled in front of the headmaster once again.

'Yeh, you've only got to grips with her once. How do you know its going to work out anyway,' said Vince.

'Look,' I said, starting to get annoyed but trying to hide it, 'It's none of your fucking business.'

Baz and Vince grabbed each other and pointed

a couple of limp wrists at me shouting 'Ooh!', in unison. I laughed at their low-rent Larry Grayson impersonations.

'Give me a fucking break. There is nothing happening this weekend anyway. Is there?'

'Harold Beaver are playing at the Bowes,' offered Vince.

'Exactly,' I said, 'If it's a toss-up between a bunk-up in Henley or another night with you lot and a band I've seen before, I'll take the sex.'

Baz and Vince looked at each other in resignation and shrugged. That was the last I heard from them about my date with Claudia. Baz sparked up a joint and we listened to Frenzy's 'Clockwork Toy' album.

After much persuasion I managed to get my old man to relinquish his iron grip on the family car keys. Early on the Saturday evening that I was due at Claudia's he cornered me in the kitchen, out of my mum's earshot, before he handed them over.

'Now listen,' he growled quietly, 'No wheel-spinning down at the station car park. Those tyres cost money.' He glanced over his shoulder to check where my Mum was, 'And no dirty stains on the car seats. You know what I mean, I don't want to explain to your mother what any sticky marks or damp patches are.'

I nodded silently, grabbed the keys and made for the door.

He shouted after me, 'And bring it back tonight! I'm going fishing tomorrow.'

The light was fading as I headed down to Henley and, after a few stops to squint at the map, I reached Claudia's after dark. As I drove up to her house I checked the address again to make sure it was the right place. It looked like a Bond villain's lair, all funny angled roofs and floor to ceiling windows. The address matched the one she had gave me so I drove through the gate and up the long drive to the house. I parked in front of one of the two double garages which were linked to the house with some sort of futuristic car port. The front door was a huge slab of pine with no handle or letterbox and I fumbled about at the side of it until my fingers hit a discreet doorbell. Eventually the door swung open silently and Claudia appeared. She had certainly not dressed down for a night in and looked great. Her thick, black quiff was immaculate and she had a bit of slap on which highlighted her natural good looks even more. She also had on a tight pair of black denims and a figure hugging white vest.

'Harry! I thought you had got lost,' she said and gave me a firm hug.

'Yeh, I was but the coppers stopped me. They don't normally see anything other than Bentleys and Rolls Royce's round here,' I joked. 'It's a bit posh this gaff isn't it?'

'Oh yeh,' was all she said and gave me a right old wet kiss. We stood in the doorway with our lips locked together and our hands stroking each other gently.

Eventually she broke off, 'C'mon, come inside.'

'Hell's teeth,' I exclaimed as I saw the vast interior of the house for the first time. It was open plan, huge and spacious with a spiral staircase, a sunken seating area and littered with all manner of designer furniture and artwork. One whole wall was covered with bookshelves. All we had in our living room was the Yellow Pages, the TV Times and a few (surprisingly smutty) Jackie Collins paperbacks.

'This is some pad Clau,' I said in an almost hushed tone.

She seemed a little embarrassed.

'My dad's an architect. He designed it himself back when I was a baby. C'mon, sit down.'

She led me by the hand into the sunken living

room. The rest of the house had gleaming wooden flooring but the seating area had a thick woolly carpet. I believe they called it shag pile back in the seventies. Maybe that was a good omen.

'So are your folks out tonight?' I asked.

'Yeh. They have gone to a concert in London.'

I did not ask but I was pretty sure that they were not off to a Chas & Dave gig or a chicken-in-a-basket night at the local social club.

'So,' she said pulling me closer to her, 'We have the place to ourselves'.

We kissed and rolled around on the couch a bit, eventually ending up on the carpet.

When we took a bit of a breather and, despite my best efforts to keep it cool, I blurted out 'I couldn't wait to see you Claudia. I've been thinking about you all week.'

'Is that right,' she said, smiling and gritting her teeth lightly in a saucy manner. 'Well I've been waiting on you Mr Powell.' She poked me playfully, 'Waiting for you to get on the phone then get down here. What kept you?'

Claudia started to tickle me and we wrestled a bit until she was on top then she leant over and gave me a kiss. As our tongues lashed together I slid my hands under her top and fondled her firm breasts through her silky bra. She pulled away and sat astride me quite abruptly then peeled off her top, unhooked her bra and revealed her full, shapely knockers. She could not have helped but notice my growing pleasure as I was smiling so much that my cheeks were aching and my cock was straining violently to break free from my denims. I reached up to touch her breasts but she moved back slightly and set to work loosening my belt then she pulled my trousers and pants off with a firm tug. She ran her fingers lightly over my wedding tackle then leaned over my crotch and placed my hard-on between her soft, warm jugs. My whole body stiffened and a wave of tingling pleasure washed over me. I thought that the fabled 'diddy ride' was simply an act of foreplay which existed in Knocker's imagination but now I was experiencing it in the flesh and it felt fantastic.

The best was yet to come as Claudia broke off from tantalising me with her tits, moved down my body even further and placed my bell-end in her hot, wet mouth. She moved all around my privates kissing and licking my balls and moving from the base of my penis to the tip. I almost fainted as this intense pleasure had me writhing on the floor with my eyes tightly shut. Then I felt her smooth thighs brush against my face as somehow she had managed to remove her trousers and pants and now had me in the classic '69' position. Her moist muff pressed against my nose urgently and I fingered it firmly then let my tongue do the business. We ground together rhythmically, furiously licking at both ends until both our bodies shook together. Claudia turned round and snuggled close to me as I lay back staring at the ceiling. I had never felt pleasure so intensely before and was almost rendered mute. All I could do was exhale slowly through my pursed lips as if I was silently whistling. Claudia giggled, 'Oh Harry, I'm sorry… I forgot to ask if you wanted a coffee.'

For the next few months, following my first visit to Claudia's house, our relationship just got better and better. Once my Dad had convinced himself that I was not using the car as a mobile knocking shop he began to lend it to me more freely and I managed to get down to see Clau two or three times a week. She also borrowed her older brother's VW Beetle occasionally and dragged herself away from the splendour of Henley to visit me in Stevenage. She met my folks, I met her parents and… blah, blah, blah, it was all going smoothly. She was smart, sexy, a great laugh and she shared the same passion for Psychobilly that I had.

She was none too shabby in all other passion departments either and whenever we were alone we went at it like Spaniards. I was actually a bit stunned upon leaving Claudia's house after my first visit as, despite grinning like a village idiot and still feeling shivers of pleasure across my body, I realised that we had not actually had full sex. I wondered if she was a foreplay maniac and our romance was destined to be nothing more than a parade of 69's and diddy rides. While that is certainly not one of the worst scenarios I could picture in my life, I was still keen to take our sex life to the next level.

I need not have worried however as during my second visit to her house, one night during the following week, she had an empty house once again and eventually got me in the bath, soaped me up and straddled me frantically. After that, the following weeks and months were a long and often adventurous series of sexual trysts. While it sounds a cliché, there was certainly more to the relationship than just endless bunk-ups. We got on well together and laughed, joked and talked for ages. With most of the girls in Stevenage that I had shagged, as soon as the deed was done I was looking to make my escape either by sneaking away from them as they slept or by making some bogus excuse to leave. With Claudia it was never like that, we were comfortable in each other's company since our first meeting.

We saw Christmas and New Year in together and as 1987 rolled around the relationship was still strong, all through the Winter months and beyond we were constantly in each other's company. All this romance took up a bit of time though, probably more than I realised, and it soon got noticed. The first night that I turned up on my own to meet the crew at the pub kickstarted a torrent of abuse.

'Well, well,' said Baz sarcastically, 'She finally let

you out on your own then?'

'What do you mean?' I immediately realised that this had been the wrong question to ask.

'Do us a favour,' sneered Vince, 'You're never out the door without her these days. You've missed three nights out and brought her along to the last four or five gigs. Has she never heard of a lad's night out?'

'Of course she has,' I fired back 'But I want to see her. It's none of your fucking business anyway. I'm going for a piss.' I could feel myself getting angry but did not want to let them see it. I took a long, leisurely slash and then went straight to the bar. By the time I got back to my seat the conversation seemed to have drifted off of my love life.

Kenny shouted over to me, 'I'm taking the van to a Scooter run up in North next weekend Harry. You up for it?'

Before I could answer, Vince jumped in, 'No point asking him, she won't be into it.'

I shouted back at him, 'For fuck's sake Vince, give it a rest. Shona and Lynne are always around. I don't hear you giving the other guys any earache.'

'Yeh, but they are just part of the furniture,' laughed Stan.

Shona dug her elbow into his ribs, 'Cheeky bastard. Just ignore them Harry. She's cool. They are all just jealous.'

Kev tried to take a bit of heat out of the argument, 'Shona's right. She is cool Harry. A tasty sort too but we hardly ever see you any more.'

Shane joined in, 'Yeh Harry, take it down a bit. You're getting in too deep, too quick. It might not last forever but we will still be here.' He obviously realised that he was sounding a bit sentimental and quickly changed his tone, 'Don't mug us off for some bird man.'

Eventually I relented. I told them that I realised that I had been seeing a bit much of my new squeeze and vowed not to 'mug them off'. I bought a round and after a few more drinks we all got up on the dance floor and fucked about to a few of the Rockabilly, Ska and Glam Rock tracks that the DJ had. When closing time was called we all stumbled home past the kebab shop. Despite the early earache, it was a great night. The whole crew together just like we had always been. I phoned Claudia as soon as I got up the next morning.

On the Sunday afternoon after my 'trial' at the pub Claudia came up to visit me. I heard the distinctive 'phut, phut' of her brother's car as I lay on the bed attempting to shake off my hangover. I could hear my old man letting her in at the front door.

'Hello love, he's upstairs in his pit. Up you go.' His tone hushed out of my Mum's earshot, 'And tell him to open a fucking window.'

Claudia was still giggling as she came into the room, 'Hi Harry, your Dad says…'

'… I heard him, I heard him. The cheeky old sod.'

She threw open a window then sat next to me on the bed and delivered a warm, wet kiss. I ran my hands over her body and squeezed her firm, shapely butt cheeks. After a few minutes of grinding together on my unmade bed we took a breather.

'So your mates were giving you a hard time last night?' asked Claudia as we lay back together on the bed.

'Oh they are just fucking jealous that they don't have their own steady birds.'

'Is that what I am now? A steady bird? Ooh, fantastic,' she replied with a sting of sarcasm.

'No, I don't… I didn't mean…' I stuttered.

'Oh calm down,' said Claudia, 'I'm only pulling your leg.'

'I know, I know but they were being a right pain

in the arse about it. It's none of their fucking business what I get up to.' I ran my fingers gently over Claudia's belly, 'Just because I've got the tastiest Psychobetty outside of the M25.'

'Psychobetty? Fuck off,' she squealed as she punched me playfully in the stomach.

We wrestled for a bit then locked lips together for another few minutes. Although my knob was bursting to get out, luckily I had kept it caged as without warning, my Mum used that special skill that all parents have - the ability to knock and open a door at the same time.

'Oh, I'm sorry,' she said. Like fuck she was sorry. 'Me and your Dad are going out for a bit. We won't be long.'

She had tacked that last bit on as some sort of veiled warning not to get up to anything too saucy. Fuck that, my sister was out as well and after the front door slammed shut I could feel a session materialising in the not too distant future.

'Listen Harry,' said Claudia as she sat up on the bed, 'I don't want to get in between you and your mates…'

'… No Claudia, you don't have to say anything. I want you to be with me when I'm out with them. I've seen those relationships where you only meet on Wednesdays and Sundays and never go out together at weekends because one or both of you have something better to do. They don't work. It's not our problem, it's theirs. No one seems to bother that Lynne and Shona are around all the time.'

'They probably just miss you not being out on your own with them. I know what you guys are like when you get together. Talking shit. You love it.'

'Well they will just have to get used to talking shit on their own.'

I stood up and pulled her off the bed gently. We stood together in the middle of the room hugging.

'I want to be with you Claudia. I've never met anyone like you. Your so special.'

I took a bit of a quick breath and my mind raced. Hold up! Special! Was that a good choice of words? A bit close to Special Brew? Maybe I should have concentrated a bit more in my English class when I was at school. I need not have worried though.

Claudia kissed me gently then spoke quietly into my ear, 'No, its you that's special.'

We stood together for a moment just holding each other and for a short period of time there was more on my mind than just my raging boner. I felt that our relationship had just nudged itself over into something more meaningful and hit upon a quick plan to seal the deal. Breaking away from her I made my way over to the record player.

'Harry!' she said, slightly shocked at my abrupt move.

'Just wait a minute Clau. One second…'

It was a bit of music that was required to put a soundtrack to this perfect moment. I flicked hastily through my records. What was I to do? Put on a Skitzo album and knock her around the room? No, this required subtlety. I remembered that Vince had left some albums for me to check out. I flicked through them. The Krewmen? Guana Batz? The Vibes? No, no, no! Chess Records' Northern Soul? Bingo, yes! I slipped it on. First track, Terry Callier's 'Ordinary Joe'. Perfect, a slow, smooth shuffler dripping with soul. As I moved away from the stereo Claudia was still looking at me a bit puzzled but she laughed as I took her in my arms and started a half-arsed waltz around the room. I held her tightly and I could feel her giggling quietly.

'You fucking smoothy.'

Terry laid it on in the background and it worked a treat. Five minutes later we were buck-naked on the bed and locked together at the hips. A further five minutes on and I was flat on my back with a dopey grin on my face while Claudia was reaching for her fags and lighter. Now that's what I call romance!

# Chapter 9
## Seaside Special

Despite the earache I got in the pub the week before I accepted Kenny's offer of a lift to the scooter run and I invited Claudia along. Kenny and Stan were happy enough with the arrangement and it only seemed to be singletons like Stan, Baz and Vince who moaned about me bringing my squeeze. They were pleasant enough when she actually turned up though… the two-faced bastards!

Claudia stayed over at my house the night before we left, only on the provision that I slept on the couch and gave her my bed. Even though my parents had lived through the swinging sixties and sexy seventies, the idea of an unmarried couple sleeping together under their roof seemed to them to be wicked beyond belief. If only they knew the amount of times that Claudia and I had rutted like wild beasts in my bedroom while they sat downstairs watching 'Antiques Roadshow'.

Kenny was round at my house early on Saturday morning, peeping his horn wildly and keen to hit the A1 North with some urgency. I knew he would be prompt so Claudia and I were packed and ready for wherever the fuck we were meant to be going. I had attended a few of these scooter rallies before and paid little attention to minor details such as the towns where the events were held. They were all in scruffy seaside resorts, mostly up North, that stank of chips, cheap hamburgers and spilt lager. I had no real interest in Scooters and went purely for the booze, the bands and the bunk-ups (if I was lucky). The evening events were usually excellent and suited my broad taste in music. There were often Psychobilly acts on the bill along with Ska groups, Punk bands and the occasional Soul legend teased out of retirement.

We were the last to be picked up and had to squeeze our way into the back of the van. Vince, Baz, Stan, Stevie, Shane and Kev were all present and Lynne and Shona were upfront once again. They looked pleased to see Claudia and obviously saw her as further female back-up against the usual excesses of farting, foul language and smut which accompanies any gathering of geezers in a van.

'So where are we off to?' I asked.

'Morecambe, mate,' shouted Kenny.

Stan sniggered. 'Hopefully I'll be spilling "more come" on some bird's tits tonight.'

Despite the fact that it was a shit joke, I knew that it was said more to test Claudia's reaction than anything else but she did not flinch and simply groaned in derision like the rest of us. She could take care of herself and it would take more than a weak spunk gag to offend her.

The rest of the trip was pretty uneventful and after what seemed like fucking ages, we finally arrived in Morecambe after endless stops for piss breaks, snacks and the traditional purchases of top-shelf dirty mags. Despite the fact that it was supposedly Spring, it was still bleedin' cold and a grey sky cloaked the town. This was the first major rally of 1987 though and the scooterist invasion of this North Western resort had created a real buzz. There had been some chin-wagging from the scootering community over the increasing number of vans and cars appearing at what was essentially a two-wheeled event but we had no intention of paying to get on to the camp site anyway and simply parked the van at the first spot we could find on the promenade. However, as the run had began the day before, our parking space was half way to fucking Blackpool.

We lit up a few joints and grabbed what booze

was left in the van to prepare ourselves for the long walk into town. Scooters were constantly cruising up and down the road and I felt my first real twinge of desire to get two-wheel burning. I could picture the freedom of hitting the road with Claudia behind me, gripping tightly and straddling my Vespa.

'I could well be into getting a scooter Clau.'

'You should Harry. You've got your car licence. Why not?'

'Would you fancy riding with me?' I asked in a sleazy tone.

She laughed and punched me on the back, 'Fuck off you pervert.'

All the way into town we passed cars and vans surrounded by empty beer cans and discarded kebab wrappers from the night before. The closer we got to town the more rally goers we spotted lounging on benches, sitting on walls or standing in small groups chatting. Although the scootering community was a varied mix of Skins, Punks, Psychobillies and ex-Mods there were also a huge number of punters driven purely by a love of scooters and with no real interest in any fashion other than a jacket covered in Paddy Smith patches and perhaps a pair of trousers with beer towels stitched on them.

Along the West promenade we were tickled to find another Clarendon Hotel. This joint was a long way from the home of the Klub Foot though and was a three star job stacked with pensioners rather than Psychobillies. The jollity was short-lived however as we discovered that getting a beer in Morecambe would prove a challenge. The first three pubs we came to were too packed with scooterists to even get in the door. Finally we found a large boozer near the seafront that had enough room for us all to squeeze into. The landlord had even made a bit of an effort to accommodate the invading scooter army and was banging out some late

1960's Ska tunes over the P.A. We made ourselves comfortable and eventually commandeered a table and set about getting seriously pissed.

A lot of folks would question why we would travel 250 miles to get boozed up in Morecambe when we could simply do the same in Stevenage then walk home at closing time. The reason is there is no contest. Why spend another weekend in the corner of some ale house surrounded by the same old local squares when we could travel to a town colonised by people with the same interests as us and have a tear-up. During trips like this we were the majority in town and all the straights, posers and small-town arseholes just had to keep their mouths shut or face a kick in the nuts. It was liberating to spend a weekend with thousands of punters who did not give a fuck what you wore, or how you styled your hair, and just wanted to get drunk, fuck about and hear some good music. I also enjoyed meeting punters from across the UK and struck up some banter with fellow rally goers whenever possible. In Stevenage, some of the town's numbskulls were loathed to even speak to people from neighbouring housing estates but generally scooterists seemed happy to mingle. I was almost ashamed that we had any reason to moan about our relatively comfy van trip when some folks came from as far as Plymouth and Aberdeen on their scoots with no regard for weather conditions or the occasionally fucked-up condition of their two-wheeled chariots.

As the beer flowed the light grey sky turned darker as night fell and the evening do grew closer. Claudia, Lynne and Shona took a break from the supping and left the pub to get some food and secure tickets for the night time entertainment. Almost as soon as they had left, Vince and Stan were on my case.

Vince prodded my side, 'Hey mate, you've been let off the chain for a bit. You can relax.'

'Yeh,' added Stan, 'Take a look at some of the

crumpet in here and see what you could have been poking. Shane and Kev look as if they are copping off already with those two Skinhead birds from Derby.'

I sighed, 'I wish you two would pack it in. It's fucking boring. I know what you are trying to do.'

'What?' said Vince in mock innocence.

'All the sex talk. Trying to embarrass Claudia.'

'That's just the way we talk,' said Stan, 'If she don't like it…'

'No, you are both dredging up all the seediest shit you can. Trying to put me on the spot. What about bringing up the story of that bird in the caravan after the Sting-Rays' gig in Nottingham.'

Stan giggled, 'What? The one that wanted the three of us to lick her ring-piece?'

'Yeh. Why the fuck did you mention that? I thought we agreed back then that we would never talk about it.'

Vince was laughing. 'Don't be an old woman, it's just a laugh.'

'I know what you're up to. It won't work. You can't scare off Clau that way. She can handle it, she's not a fucking convent girl.'

'Alright, alright. Keep your fucking hair on,' said Vince, 'We are only pissing about.' He nodded to Stan, 'Let's get the beers in.'

I had seen this happen before when any of the guys had a new girlfriend and, to be honest, I had participated in it myself and witnessed a few girls fail to make a return appearance after a night out with our crew. It was coming back to bite me in the ass though and now that I was the focus of attention it was a bit wearing.

The girls eventually returned and told us that the evening event was almost sold out but they had managed to secure tickets. After a few more beers we left the pub and headed for the venue. The scooters were long gone but the scooterists were out in force. A sea of punters in pilot jackets, jeans, boots and army trousers washed through every pub, take-away and off-licence in town. Above the shouting, banter and chanting occasional roars would erupt when people were obviously meeting up with their mates or other scooterists that they had encountered at previous rallies.

Shane and Kev broke away from our group and made their way to the beach with the girls from Derby. Obviously they had something else on their minds other than cockle picking but it seemed pretty miserable weather for a beach front bunk-up. Then again, once you get the horn these things do not seem to bother you. I once shagged a girl from Letchworth at the back of a Stevenage chippy one New Year's Night and although there were almost icicles stuck to my arse, my nob was as warm as a freshly cooked hot-dog.

The thought of all this was getting me a bit randy so I caught up with Claudia and gave her a bit of a hug as we walked along the street. I also let my hand slip down and gave her firm arse cheek a squeeze.

'What are you up to?' she asked.

'Eh, what do you mean?' I feigned innocence but I was already thinking of how I could get my Hampton dipped before sunrise.

Luckily we were all well pissed before we got to the do as inside the venue the bar was four deep and each of the punters seemed to be ordering enough drinks to last them the whole evening. This left a bit more time for dancing and we all took a turn at shaking it on the dance floor at various points in the evening. Claudia in particular was out on the floor almost continuously and that was the first time that I noticed how well she had mastered that particular Northern Soul shuffle. It always amused me to see even the most hulking brutes skip lightly across the floor to the Northern sound and it also left me a bit jealous as my attempts to trip the light fantastic were mostly clumsy. There was plenty wrecking throughout the night though so I consoled myself that that was where my talents lay.

Despite the great music and good atmosphere I still had an itch that needed to be scratched and I was determined to get sorted. I managed to persuade Kenny to part with the keys of the van and, still sporting a semi-hard on that refused to go away, I coaxed Claudia out of the venue. She was not overly keen to make sweet love at that moment but grudgingly accompanied me along the promenade to where the creaky Transit was parked. I was certainly far more pissed than Claudia was and convinced that I could take her to the peak of sexual ecstasy on that cold, April night. Once she got in the passion wagon I was sure she would share my desires.

'If you think I am bunking down in that you can fuck right off!'

Claudia was surveying the mess of discarded sleeping bags, empty beer cans and well-thumbed porn mags which littered the back of the van. I had to admit that, even in my pissed condition, it did not look too inviting and I felt that any attempt to persuade her otherwise would completely jeopardise any chance of a shag.

'Let's just sit here for a bit,' I suggested as we sat in the front seat and I attempted to slide my hand onto her bare knockers.

'Oh Harry, come on. Let's get back to the dance.'

I tried to silence her with a kiss and moved my hands down to her belt buckle. She offered no resistance and I managed to slip my hand down the front of her pants and on to her warm pussy. Her slice was moist and I suspected that some form of romance might be possible over the front seats of the van.

'Harry. This is ridiculous.'

'Oh come on, just lie back on the passenger side a little.'

She giggled slightly, 'You are insatiable.'

'I need you Claudia.'

'Yeh. I know what you need,' said Claudia sarcastically, 'And I don't think much of your choice of venue.'

Claudia lay back and I tugged at her tight jeans which eventually slid off along with her underwear. She winced slightly.

'Hurry up. Its fucking freezing.'

I felt a brief twinge of guilt as I realised that this was a none too romantic tryst but desire was driving me crazy and I pulled down my trousers and scants just enough to let my straining poker out then prodded about in the dark as I attempted to sink it into her hot lovebox.

'That's not it,' tutted Claudia impatiently as she reached down and guided my nob into its desired destination.

After some brief strokes Claudia let out a gasp of exasperation.

'Harry. Get off. This is no good, my back is stretched over the gap in the seats. You lie down instead.'

We struggled to swap places in the confined space but eventually I lay on the chairs with Claudia on top straddling my manhood. She managed to get a strong, sexy rhythm going but the pleasure of the rogering was tempered with the pain of the handbrake and gearstick jamming into my back and arse respectively. I shot my bolt all too soon and Claudia lifted herself off my wilted boner with something approaching anger and annoyance.

'Can we please get back to the venue now that you have satisfied your animal urges.'

'Hold up. I'll come with you,' came a voice from the back of the van as Vince emerged from beneath a sleeping bag.

Claudia threw me a look of pure disgust, pulled her trousers and boots back on and stormed off into the night slamming the door behind her.

'Cheers Vince,' I shouted.

'Sorry mate. Look put that shrivelled thing away and let's go after her.'

As I pulled my gear back on I realised that Vince did not quite gather how serious the incident had been.

'That reminds me Harry. Do you think they sell winkles up here?'

We caught up with Claudia before she reached the venue. I apologised profusely and assured her that Vince only woke up as we were putting our clothes back on. It took some persuading to make her believe that I had not orchestrated the whole thing as some sort of kinky, voyeuristic threesome. To his credit, Vince explained that he had simply crashed out in the van after leaving the dance early and only came round just before he heard us talk about leaving. Personally, I would not have put it past him to have had a secret wank while Claudia and I were at it but she seemed to believe him. Just before we went back into the hall, Claudia grabbed me by the jacket and pulled me close to her.

'You have got a lot of making up to do, so get me a drink then meet me on the dance floor.'

True to her word she refused to let me off the dance floor for the rest of the night and by 3am my feet ached as much as the bruises on my back and arsehole.

The punters at the evening do had gradually been slipping away all evening but there was still a very sizable mob ejected from the venue at the end of the night. After a mass exodus to whatever fast-food joints were still open, most folks drifted back to the camp site. We were all present and, clutching chips, kebabs and other grease-soaked delicacies, we gradually made our way back to our four-wheeled accommodation. Even Shane and Kev returned, having ditched the Derby girls, and they were giving us a stroke-by-stroke explanation about what they had got up to. When we got to the van the conversation started to die quickly as everyone struggled to get a sleeping bag and enough space to bed down in but odd snippets of humour, abuse and singing punctuated the silence.

At about five in the morning everyone in the van was starting to calm down and it started to go quiet, just in time as Kenny in particular seemed pretty pissed off with all the chat and giggling. I snuggled up to Claudia but could not even stretch my legs out as every part of the van's floor was covered in sweaty bodies. Cold condensation was building on the roof and starting to drip down on us all. Despite the fact that it was Spring it felt like Winter, especially as the booze began to wear off and the familiar sting of my bruised arms was making itself felt after the occasional bouts of wrecking which had went on earlier in the night.

Just before I drifted off to sleep there was a massive commotion as someone started struggling to get out of the van while cursing and obviously in some pain. I thought it was someone with a bad case of cramp and noticed that it was Vince as he burst out the back door and ran off.

'For fuck's sake!' yelled Kenny. 'What's going on? And shut that fucking door.'
Claudia was giggling furiously and her body was shaking silently.

'What's so funny?' I whispered.

'It was Vince. He tried to slip his cock into my hand to shock me.'

'What?' I yelled, 'The dirty bastard. I'll fucking do him over.'

He had been winding us up all day and this was

the final straw.

'Jesus Christ,' shouted Kenny, 'Will you fucking belt up Powell or get out.'

'Harry, calm down,' said Claudia in a hushed tone, 'I sorted it, its ok.'

'What did you do?'

'I scratched his knob with my fingernail then dipped it in that pot of kebab sauce that was left over.'

My body ached with laughter as I tried to keep the volume to a minimum but the thought of Vince struggling to find somewhere to wash his chilli sauce soaked tool was just too hilarious. It served him right, the liberty-taking bastard. I held Claudia tightly and kissed her gently once I had ceased laughing.

'You're a wicked woman Miss Quigley but I love you.'

She said nothing but kissed me back.

After a satisfying breakfast at one of Morecambe's greasiest spoons we drove back to Stevenage and all the way there Vince received merciless abuse. We took to singing 'Hot Knob' to the tune of Rod Stewart's 'Hot Legs' and every time he tried to have an inconspicuous scratch at his aching dick the chanting started again. He took it in good humour though and obviously felt pretty embarrassed by his cock-waving antics. Although to many outsiders placing your bell-end in an unsuspecting girl's hand seems one step away from a sex attack, we all knew he was simply testing Claudia's acceptance of our blokeish behaviour. The truth was that all weekend most of my mates wanted to know if Claudia would fit in as snugly as Lynne and Shona or forever remain an outsider. Would she blush and take offence at our low-brow behaviour or dig in and give as good as she got. There was no doubt that she had passed with flying colours.

'I'm sorry Vince. I thought it was your thumb.'

Claudia roared with laughter and stamped her

boots on the floor of the van.

Vince tried to laugh it off but he was obviously tiring of the teasing.

'Oh, I really am sorry mate,' said Claudia, 'I actually thought you were trying to slip me the remains of Stan's sausage supper.'

The laughter roared again and I watched Claudia slap hands with Shona and Lynne in a victorious 'high-five'. Her eyes were sparkling, her cheeks glowing red with constant giggling and a beautiful smile beamed across her face. She was comfortable and at ease along with everyone else. I could see that she was no longer just 'Harry's bird' but part of the crew.

# Chapter 10
# Self-Destruction Blues

The Psychobilly scene in England had began to get relatively established with regular rocking available across London. And the rest of the country. Stevenage also had its own home-grown talent, not only well-known Indie types such as Fields of the Nephilim and Stan Stammers from Theatre of Hate, but also Klub Foot regulars The Pharaohs and The Sting-Rays originated from just up the road in leafy Letchworth. Stevenage' long-running town centre venue The Long Ship occasionally allowed some alternative acts to play within their walls but the surest guarantee of a good night of live music could be found at the Bowes Lyon House on St. Georges Way. Although we thought of the venue as exclusive to our generation my dad remembered going to see The Who there once when he was a young Mod type back in 1966. This was the one place in town where a good selection of Indie bands could be found and the management usually understood that the occasional bout of wrecking did not constitute a bar-room brawl.

By some rare twist of fate, the night that Knocker made his first visit back home from Germany coincided with a King Kurt gig at the Bowes so none of us had any excuse for not being there to welcome him home. We were already in the club before Knocker. The flash bastard could easily have come with us earlier but he seemed to want to build his appearance into some kind of event so we obliged with a big homecoming cheer when he eventually arrived. The cunt had only been away for six months but it was good to see him again. The club was buzzing and the DJ was on top form knocking out a selection of Psychobilly, Rockabilly and Indie tracks. Knocker made a show of his recent earnings and immediately pulled out a fairly large wad of cash to get the first round in. He had obviously spent a bit on his clobber as well and he was sporting a fine new pair of black leather creepers along with what looked like some meaningful brand of jeans. I knew some Rockabilly guys who were deadly serious about what brand of jeans they wore but I had always bought the cheapest ones I could from Millets then simply added a splash of bleach on them and badgered my mum into taking them in to 14" bottoms.

Once Knocker had done the rounds and spoken to everyone, I introduced him to Claudia who had been away in the bogs with Lynne and Shona doing whatever girls do in the Ladies loo.

'Knocker, this is Clau. Clau this is my mate Knocker. Just back from Deutschland.'

'You alright love?' said Knocker casually but I immediately noticed a flash of recognition between them.

Claudia said 'Hi,' but nothing more and could barely keep her eyes off the floor.

King Kurt were about to come on so I said no more about it but I immediately knew that there was something wrong. The gig, for what it was, lasted for about five songs before the club's management got cold feet over the band's legendarily messy onstage antics and the way they were driving the crowd into an increased frenzy. With the gig drawn to a premature close we were all pretty pissed off but my night was about to get a whole lot worse.

Clau was keeping herself to herself and generally gravitating towards Lynne and Shona for most of the night. She was not avoiding me but anytime she spoke to me I got the feeling that she was pretty apprehensive over something even though she denied it. As a result, I was pretty sullen for the most of the evening and it did not go unnoticed.

'Cheer up you moody cunt,' said Vince as he flicked the head of his lager at me.

'Fuck off,' was as much wit as I could muster in reply.

'Oi, calm down,' said Baz as he noticed the first sign of trouble brewing.

'Yeh,' said Vince quietly. 'It's not me that was fucking your bird.'

My patience snapped in an instant and I kicked the table straight at Vince, managing to soak everyone else in the process. I leapt across the shattered beer glasses and grabbed him by the throat with both hands. Everyone was on their feet and we were dragged apart in seconds but I was still focused on Vince who I felt was responsible for all the dark thoughts that were in my mind. I lashed out at him with my boot but Knocker and Baz held me back firmly.

'C'mon now Harry. Fucking calm down,' said Baz as he pulled my arm firmly behind my back.

All I could feel was a rush of hate towards Vince as I yelled, 'What do you mean? What do you mean?'

Vince was equally furious and struggling violently with Kenny and Stan to get back at me.

'It wasn't me you crazy prick, it was Knocker. He got first dibs on her back at that Klub Foot party. You were there you dozy bastard!'

I stopped struggling immediately. They say a car crash hits you in slow motion and that is exactly how I felt. I could see Vince's leering face then I looked at Knocker as his eyes drifted to the floor. I remembered how I had interrupted Knocker mid-shag at that party in Hammersmith. I remembered the tasty bird with the purple quiff who had stormed past me with her clothes in her hands. Naked and defiled by one of my mates. It was Claudia. They all knew and even at the back of my subconscious I must have known. Baz and Knocker loosened their grip on me and I turned to face Knocker.

'Listen Harry,' he said calmly, 'It was before you met her and if you start anything right now I will fucking drop you to the floor.'

'I'm sure you would you flash bastard,' I said quietly and pushed past him towards the exit. Claudia had missed the fracas but as she saw me start to leave she tried to grab my arm.

'Harry…' she pleaded.

'Fuck off,' was all she got in reply.

My head was buzzing as I walked a short distance from the pub and flopped down onto a park bench. I had a peculiar feeling of anger, disappointment, guilt and lager swilling inside me. I could still hear the throb of music from the pub. I felt a hand on my shoulder as Claudia sat down beside me.

'What the fuck was that all about?' she asked.

Don't play the innocent with me,' I spat back. 'You knew. You all knew!'

'Look, what exactly are you trying to say here?' said Claudia angrily. 'Stop going round the houses and tell me what is bothering you.'

I could feel my face turning a darker shade of red. 'It was you that night after the Klub Foot. In the bathroom with Knocker.'

'In the bathroom? What are you talking about?' she said.

'In the bog at that party. Getting fucked from behind by my mate Knocker.'

Realisation seemed to hit her. She paused for a moment as she stared at the ground. 'It might have been. I don't know… So what?'

'So what?' I screeched, 'How many times have you had it doggy style in the toilet with guys you have just met?'

Claudia was furious but tears were starting to well up in her eyes, 'I've lost count. Its been that fucking many. What is it to you anyway, it was before we met.'

'We met back then, I walked in on you. You didn't even have the decency to lock the fucking door,' I screamed.

Claudia looked shocked as if I had just slapped her across the face then she screamed back.

'Decency! Who the fuck are you? Mary Whitehouse? How dare you talk to me like that. What about all the birds that you shagged before we met? That does not bother me. Since I met you there has only been you. Why does it bother you who I was with before?'

Without thinking I blurted back, 'But it was my mate.'

Claudia again looked shocked, this time at my idiocy, 'But I didn't even know you. I didn't know he was your mate. Are you fucking stupid?' Her voice was weakening and tears filled her eyes, 'You didn't know about this before we met. Why should it bother you now?'

In retrospect, that would have been the perfect time to calm down, realise that what had happened in her past was long gone, apologise and take her in my arms. Instead I opted for an explosive relationship-buster of mammoth proportions.

'If I had known you were such a slag I wouldn't have went near you!'

Claudia let out a gasp as if I had stabbed her in the chest. The tears fell from her eyes but she still looked beautiful. She put her face in her hands and her huge sobs shook her shoulders. Even then an instant apology might have went some way to easing the massive blow that I had dealt her but, like a fucking arrogant arsehole, I sat still - shaking with anger and regret. Claudia rubbed her eyes and looked at me as if I was something she had found stuck to the rim of a toilet.

She shook her head slowly, stood up, and growled, 'You fucking arsehole.'

Even then she paused for a moment looking for some sign of my regret but I sat rooted to the bench. She did not say anything else and began walking away. Here we go! Last chance to save the best relationship I have ever experienced with a girl that means so much to me. No! My subconscious seemed determined to crush our six-month romance on the rocks. I said nothing then got up and walked in the opposite direction.

As I walked away I felt a raging anger build inside me. Not a sense of loss or guilt or sadness, just pure anger. Anger at myself for being such an arsehole. I was walking between three blocks of flats and I noticed a two-storey public car park at my side. The lights around it were long smashed and only the most reckless motorist would use it now. It looked as if it would be a suitable place to park up an old banger and one such rust bucket was visible on the ground floor. As I walked towards it I grabbed a large stone from a nearby bit of landscaping and launched it towards the windscreen. For some reason it simply bounced off and inflamed my impotent anger even more. As I got closer to the car I noticed a long metal pole lying amongst some old tyres and oil cans. I picked it up and put the windscreen in with one whack then moved on to the headlights, the bonnet, the wing mirrors, the side windows. On and on, lost in a one man destruction derby and filled with images of Knocker slipping his pork sword into my sweet Claudia.

'Hey, you Punk tosser. What are you doing?'

A voice broke through my cloud of rage. I looked up and saw three poser types standing at the entrance to the car park. My anger must have really clouded my judgement as, instead of looking for an escape route, I ran towards them yelling.

'Fuck you, you trendy cunts.'

A little anger can only get you so far and, though it often worked for David Banner, it did not do me any fucking good. Although I managed to land a few good punches they were seasoned scrappers and spent an enjoyable evening kicking me up and down the car park. Eventually they left me lying amongst the broken glass that I had created myself. I could feel the familiar warm sensation of blood on my face and each breath I took made my ribs ache. I had been in this position before but this time it did not feel like a kicking. It felt like self-destruction.

# Chapter 11
# Here We Are Nowhere

While the recovery following the beer bottle attack outside The Long Ship garnered a few visitors, after my car park pasting no one came round or even phoned. I do not suppose that putting a downer on Knocker's first visit home and coming to blows with Vince added to my popularity but as the days passed I started to feel a little resentment building and the sting of having pushed Claudia away only added to it. Baz had phoned a few times but my mum had taken the calls and I had yet to call him back. I assumed that I would be as welcome as a fart in a spacesuit but I made no real attempt to actually find out. I just lay in bed for days until I could afford to cough without unleashing a barrage of pain from my bruised ribs.

I was also suffering from a painful dose of earache as my mum took advantage of my bed-ridden condition and used the opportunity to regularly badger me about running around with 'skinheads'. It was a common misconception amongst oldies and squares who were ignorant about Psychobilly style. Despite the fact that most of us had fairly large flat-tops and quiffs, few Joe Soaps could see beyond our boots, pilot jackets and partly-shaved heads. They still saw the faithful folk devil of the Skinhead, whose negative media portrayal has been a staple of the press since 1969. As well as my Mum's moaning, I received a letter from the council informing me that the extension to my YTS would not be renewed and after a further two weeks sick pay my contract would be 'terminated'. I was sure that Bernie would have little to do with the decision, and probably be a little embarrassed about it, but talk about lucky white heather… everything I was touching was turning to shit.

As I lay there covered in a sweaty quilt and an extra layer of self-pity, I had no enthusiasm for anything and my beloved collection of Psychobilly records just sat in the corner gathering dust. I heard Pamela Donald's voice in the hallway one night, as she followed my sister into her room, and half hoped that she might slip in to visit me with the option of sliding between the sheets for a quick sympathy fuck. It never happened and even my once healthy wanking regime was on the wane. Something had to change.

I have never been one to work out any great life plan and since leaving school I had simply drifted into whatever vocation came my way. There was no great career move planned but during one of my many days scratching my arse in my sick bed I came across an advert in the local rag for an 'exhibition assistant' for a company down in London and the pay looked pretty healthy. I had done some work of this kind for the council but more importantly the position offered accommodation as part of the package. It was just the opportunity I needed to escape from moaning mothers, Judas mates and ex-girlfriends. It was also what I needed to rouse me from my pit of depression.

A fortnight later I had completed an interview and, despite my still bruised face, I had secured the job. I landed in a one bedroom flat in Walton-On-Thames so quickly that it left my mum gasping over how quickly 'her boy' had deserted her. Most of the work was in London but the company was based in Walton, a leafy suburb so far west from the centre of the metropolis that it almost touched the M25. The job involved erecting and dismantling exhibition stands at venues and function rooms across London and the hours were long but I dived in with great enthusiasm. It was my Foreign Legion, I was working 'to forget'. It certainly served its purpose as over the next few months I forgot about pretty much everything apart from working, eating, sleeping and looking with growing contentment at my growing bank balance. I also regained the power to wank and splashed some of my cash on a new video and a fair collection of VHS smut.

Something which had also slipped my mind was paying attention to my once-impressive Psychobilly barnet. I had little time to spare teasing my quiff into action and it flopped down to something resembling a side-parting as the shaven parts grew back in. It did not seem to matter anymore as most days I was only ever wearing my company uniform from dawn till dusk then flaking out. The guys I worked with were decent enough but we had little in common other than enjoying a pint or two at knocking off time. All they talked about was football and their lives seemed to revolve around their local boozer when they were not at work. For almost six months I lived a pretty solitary existence but it did not really bother me. The workload was so constant that the time just drifted by. I enjoyed living on my own and the sick, dull feeling that I got in my stomach every time I thought of Claudia began to fade.

My only contact with Stevenage was an occasional phone call to my mum to assure her that I was not starving to death or living in squalor. I got a bit of gossip in return; my sister was still a cheeky bitch but hanging around with a 'nice' crowd and Pamela Donald was pregnant. I shit myself a bit when I heard that but after asking a few questions about female fertility and checking some dates in my diary, I realised that I was out of the frame. It seemed that Baz had also been in touch but as I had no phone at the flat all my mum could do was let me know. I still did not phone him back though.

I received the news that we had a job on at Hammersmith with mixed emotions. Obviously I still remembered the sheer buzz of the nights we had spent at the Klub Foot but it was also nearby where I had witnessed Claudia being manhandled by Knocker and, even though that night was over a year ago, it still gave me a small sting of anger and regret. We passed the Clarendon Hotel on the first day of the job and it did not look much without its lights on or a throng of excited Psychobillies outside. It still looked active though and a few posters for gigs flapped around its tatty exterior.

The job itself was more of the same - build it up, pull it down a few days later and try not to act too abusively to the wankers that were paying for it. Pandering to the demands of some of the clients was starting to peeve me as most of them believed themselves to be interior designers and seemed to forget that our exhibition stands were really no more than glorified market stalls designed to sell their products and services. The amount of times I had built a stand to the client's original plan, adjusted it for them, then ended up reverting to Plan A on their insistence was beginning to piss me off.

The Hammersmith exhibition was a recruitment fair at a hotel near the Klub Foot and it took fucking ages to clear the hall on the final day which resulted in us still dismantling the stand well into Saturday evening. As I was loading up the van I noticed four young Psychobilly types walking along the street necking bottles of Merrydown and pissing about. They were a bit younger than me but had finely sculpted quiffs and the usual uniform of boots and bleached jeans. Their white T-shirts boasted familiar names. The Meteors, Guana Batz and Torment but one had a Klingonz T-shirt. I had never heard of them, I must be losing touch. As they passed me without looking I shouted out to them as I sussed they were heading towards the Klub Foot.

'Who's playing tonight lads?'

They kept walking and one shouted back, 'Spandau Ballet's tomorrow night… wanker.'

The cheeky cunt. If I had been in the wrecking pit I would have bounced him round the floor. But I was not in the wrecking pit. I caught a look at myself in a shop window - jeans, polo shirt, trainers and a haircut that was going nowhere in its blandness. Average. Since that bust-up at Knocker's homecoming I had lost everything. Not just my mates and girlfriend but also my style and my love of Psychobilly. I had dropped everything like a spoilt kid just because things had not went my way. Not only that, I had left my record collection behind like an ugly girl at a wedding. Psychobilly was behind everything I had; friends, great experiences, good times and self-esteem. I had ignored it and lost everything. Now I was just like everybody else - a fucking nothing! I started throwing the gear into the van with a fury. I was disgusted with myself.

My anger following the job at Hammersmith did not fade. All day Sunday I prowled restlessly around the flat working out a plan of attack. No sooner had I phoned in sick on Monday morning than I was banging on the door of the local barber's shop, desperate to rid myself of my shapeless barnet. Although Walton appeared to be a Psychobilly-free zone, the geezer understood my instructions perfectly and I emerged thirty minutes later with an impressive pomp once more. My period in exile had one benefit as now a ten inch quiff stuck out thick and proud as it gradiated down to four inches at the back with a razor sharp number one at the back and sides. It looked good even though it was only held together with a few squirts of some ancient hairspray which was knocking around the salon. Once I set about it with some gel and a hair dryer it would look even sharper. As I walked down the street I noticed a few people staring at me. This was better. Before now I had been inconspicuous and blended into the background. Fuck that, I felt proud once again of my Psychobilly style.
I liberated some cash from my account

and caught the train into London. My first stop was Kensington market where I stocked up on T-shirts, a new pilot jacket and a cracking pair of black suede crepes. I left the shapeless gear that I had been wearing behind in a changing room as I would not be needing it. Next up was a trip to Millets for some tartan shirts and a new pair of steel toe-capped Doc Martens. I even had a good scout through the record shops and picked up a few Meteor's albums which I had missed and the latest Torment LP. When I got home that night I was buzzing more than I had been in ages. It soon fizzled out though when I realised that I was still in Walton on my own. My whole time here had served its purpose, my head was clear and I knew where I wanted to be… back in the wrecking pit with my mates. I could have fucked it all up though and I was not sure that my return would be welcomed. It was time to get back in touch with the New Town.

'Baz? It is me, Harry.'

'Harry you old pervert. How you doing? Where the fuck have you been?' Baz voice sounded genuinely excited over the phone.

'I'm in Walton.'

'Yeh, yeh, I know that. Your mum told me but what's with the silence. Why the big disappearing act?'

I did not really know myself but made a half-hearted explanation, 'I just had to get away mate. All that shit with Claudia… fucking up Knocker's night out… I just felt that I was better off out of it.'

'Piss off,' laughed Baz, 'That was all forgotten about the next morning. We've had worst bust-ups than that within the crew. Remember that night when Shane and Kev shaved Stan's pubes off when he fell asleep at their gaff?'

'No, it was my pubes,' I interrupted.

'Yeh, yeh. You're right… it was something else.

Yeh, they pulled his cock out and painted it with blue emulsion when he was crashed out. Well he went fucking mental when he woke up. He had only just started going out with Shona and she was there. Remember?'

'He hit Shane with a bottle didn't he?' I asked as I remembered the incident although I had not been there that night.

'Yeh, that is how he got that cut over his eye, and when they both went to hospital Kev tried to get off with Shona. When Stan heard about it in the morning he went fucking mental and had a go at Kev as well.'

I laughed to myself as I had never heard the full story.

'Anyway,' continued Baz, 'It was all forgotten about in no time, just like your crack-up at Knocker's do. Everyone has been asking about you. They can't work it out. Did you get a kicking that night from some casuals?'

'Yeh,' I said, 'Later on, up at that car park near the flats on Rockingham Way.'

'I heard a bit of that from your sister… hey, talking of that. She said that you nearly got that tasty sort Pamela Donald up the stick. You kept that quiet, you sneaky bastard!'

I let out something between a sly giggle and a dirty laugh like Sid James, 'Listen. Its not mine. I've worked it out but I did get a bunk-up one night back at mine when she was a bit pissed.'

'You saucy cunt, she is as tasty as fuck,' gasped Baz. 'Anyway, when are you coming home? Knocker and me are going out tonight.'

'Is Knocker back again?'

'He has been back for fucking weeks. He got deported. Arrested at a police raid on a brothel then kicked out of the fatherland. Turns out he was getting plenty fanny over there but he was paying for it. He blew all his cash and now he is back home and signing on. The flash bastard.'

My body shook with laughter. 'Baz. Stop it mate, you're cracking me up.'

'Listen Harry get yourself back. Everyone wants to see you. Demented are playing the Bowes on Saturday.'

I knew from that moment that my long days of stand building and short nights alone in Walton were over. It was time to hand in my notice.

'What are the chances of Kenny getting that shitty old van down here this week to pick up me and all my crap?'

'It's done mate,' yelped Baz, 'I'll sort it.'

'That's fucking great,' I replied as I felt a warm rush of excitement hit me.

Baz paused for a section, 'Just one thing Harry.' It sounded ominous. 'Vince has been seeing Claudia for about a month now. They seem pretty serious.'

The sleazy bastard, was my first thought but as I pondered over the news I realised that I did not feel so bad about it.

'When did that happen?'

'One night after a gig at the Headstone. Only Stan and Vince went so Claudia put them up at her gaff afterwards. Stan ended up playing gooseberry.'

I paused for thought but could not really think of much to say.

'Fair enough mate.'

'You sure?' questioned Baz.

I paused again but I still did not feel to peeved, upset, angry… or anything else. 'Yeh of course', was my only answer.

Baz' tone brightened up immediately, 'Alright then. I'll get on the blower to Kenny. Back to the New Town. Can you handle it?'

I realised that it was not just my family and friends that I had missed but Stevenage itself.

To say my Mum was glad to see me back home was a bit of an exaggeration. Despite her constant reassurance that 'your room will always be ready for you' etc. whenever we spoke on the phone, she nearly wet the bed when Kenny's tatty van pulled up outside the house and we began dragging my belongings back into the house. When she heard that not only was I back home for good but also jobless, my big return home was greeted less than enthusiastically.

'You back then? I knew it wouldn't last,' sniped Yvonne.

'Yes dear sister,' I said sarcastically, 'Wonderful to see you too.'

She laughed, 'Better get Mum to stock up on the bog rolls again.'

'Alright Son,' was all I got from my Dad. He barely looked at me as he was watching yet another episode of Dempsey & Makepeace.

Nothing had changed in my room, so much so that even some dried up balls of post-wanking toilet paper were still present under my bed gathering dust. I was good to be back though and I felt that I somehow had to mark the occasion. Before I unpacked, I pulled 'Zorch Factor One' from my album collection, blew the dust from my stereo and put on 'The Source' by Torment. Then I had a toss.

# Chapter 12
# Never Lose It

On my first Saturday back in Stevenage I spent most of the day with Baz. We got some cans from the off-licence and sat in his room all afternoon, drinking and listening to records. Despite the buzz of being back in familiar territory I was still apprehensive about meeting the rest of the crew. For this reason, I dragged Baz around a few pubs prior to making an appearance at the Demented gig. He eventually grew tired of my reticence and forced me out of the door, 'Sup up mate, fucking Demented will already be on now.'

As we got close to the club I could hear the dull thud of Demented Are Go coming from the inside. Short bursts of drumming, the singer's guttural vocals and that steady slap of double-bass. As we got rubbed down by the bouncers I could start to make out a distinctive, deep twangy guitar. Just inside the door I could see a smattering of Psychobillies milling around. As I paid my entrance fee I noticed a few familiar faces and gave them a nod. Baz slapped me on the back just before we entered the hall, 'Good to be back, eh mate?'

I smiled but said nothing.

As we went through the doors we were plunged into darkness and I could feel a heavy blast of warm, sweaty air covering me. I could see the band on stage but the bright coloured stage lights combined with the darkness of the hall rendered the dance floor as no more than a heaving mass of bodies. Gradually, as my eyes became accustomed to the dark I began to recognise some faces who I knew and then I spotted my mates. Kenny Priest, Shane and Kev dragged me towards them, slapping me on the back and yelling good-natured abuse into my ear. Stan and Stevie joined in on the huddle then Shona and Lynne broke through and tried to squeeze the life out of me. Knocker appeared out of the shadows and glared at me.

'Here to spoil another party are you Powell?' he growled.

He seemed intent on spoiling my night but I spoke to him calmly even though I was in no mood for any of his shit.

'Look Knocker, that was all just a big mistake but if you want to start something...'

He was staring me down and then his face finally cracked into a smile.

'Aah!' he yelled. 'Got you! Reeled you in like a fucking trout.' He shook my hand furiously and slapped my back, 'Good to see you mate. I've got some tales to tell you from Europe.' Chances are they would be full of shit but I could not wait to hear them.

Baz introduced me to a few new Psychobilly geezers who seemed to be part of our crowd and then he yelled in my ear, 'I told you that you had to come back. You can't leave all this behind.'

Demented reached the end of their song and the crowd went wild. It was then that I noticed Vince and Claudia near the front of the stage. They saw the gathering around me and walked over. The rest of the crew all seemed to take a little step back.

Vince held out his hand a bit warily, 'Harry?'

I shook his hand firmly, 'Cheers Vince.'

Claudia reached forward and squeezed my arm, 'Great to see you Harry.'

She still looked beautiful but it was good to see her without feeling a cruel stab of jealousy in my guts.

'It's good to see you Clau.'

Seeing all my mates together again gave me a real buzz but the crackle of excitement I felt in the venue was even more powerful. The band had launched into the distinctive guitar intro from 'Satan's Rejects' and I took a deep breath and drew the feeling into my guts once again. It was the Psychobilly disease and I had a bad dose of it. Once again, I was back amongst my Psychobilly brothers and sisters and I had never felt better. The thing is that Psychobilly is far more than just a fad or a fashion. You never lose it, it is part of you. It is what separates you from all the faceless losers on the street who do not believe in anything.

    I could see a pit of wildly flaying bodies in front of me and I pushed my way to the heart of it. Elbows, knuckles, shoulders and fists were flying everywhere. Punters were dropping like flies then being dragged back to their feet. Flecks of blood were hitting my T-shirt and people were smiling and whooping wildly with bloody smiles and burst noses. A mountainous fat geezer with a Restless tattoo appeared in front of me and as he lurched back sharply one of his big, Bluto-like, forearms slammed across my forehead. The familiar blackout curtain of unconsciousness fell over me as I crumpled to the floor. I could feel my mates dragging me away from the many pairs of crunching boots on the dance floor and I could still hear the band kicking up a glorious, unholy racket. I heard someone calling my name but gradually all the sounds of the club swirled together as they faded into silence. As that clumsy fat bastard's knockout blow took effect I could feel only a warm glow. It was great to be back.

**The End**

# Also available by this author

## HELL'S BENT ON ROCKIN': A History of Psychobilly

Published by CHERRY RED BOOKS
ISBN 9781901447804

Despite being starved of the oxygen of mainstream music press attention for over 25 years, Psychobilly has thrived in the underground, building a network of fiercely loyal followers and producing a huge number of bands who each peddle their own brand of the genre.

'Hell's Bent On Rockin' follows the scene from its initial boom in the early 1980's, through the lean years of the late 1990's to the current 'Psychobilly Renaissance' of the 21st Century where the genre looks dangerously close to crossing over into the mainstream alternative scene, particularly in America where Psychobilly has experienced a recent rebirth on a very large scale.

The book explores the roots of Psychobilly, not only in Rockabilly and Punk but also in 1960's Garage Punk, Glam Rock, revival Rock 'n' Roll and Heavy Metal. It focuses on key pioneers of the scene such as The Meteors, Guana Batz, King Kurt, The Krewmen, Frenzy and Demented Are Go then looks in detail at the bands which followed in their wake all across the UK, Ireland and Western Europe.

As followers of Psychobilly are intensely loyal and as much a part of the scene as the bands, the book also includes first hand testimonials from a number of music fans detailing how they first became hooked by the Psychobilly bug. 'Hell's Bent On Rockin' also focuses on the key record labels, promoters, fanzines and websites which are an integral part of the genre.

This book covers the careers and key releases from hundreds of Psychobilly bands across the globe including regions where the Psychobilly disease has also spread such as Japan, Russia, Australia, Mexico and South America. It also details the fashion, haircuts and tattoos which give Psychobilly its style and looks at a variety of related music genres such as Neo-Rockabilly, Trash, Garage punk and Speedrock.

240 pages with over 150 photographs & illustrations.

## LET'S WRECK: Psychobilly Flashbacks From The Eighties & Beyond

Published by STORMSCREEN PRODUCTIONS
ISBN 0954624904

The wrecking-est, rockin-est bastard offspring of rockabilly & punk, PSYCHOBILLY is the music genre that refuses to die despite being ignored by the mainstream music business and press for over two decades.

Kicked into action in the early 1980's by UK psycho-pioneers such as The Meteors, King Kurt, The Guana Batz and The Sharks, the Psychobilly sound has evolved and mutated into a global phenomenon as its sickness spreads across continents and takes its grip on the 21st Century.

LET'S WRECK is the story of one man's trip through British Psychobilly, from a spotty teen sporting his first flat-top in the early 1980's to a balding rocker of today. This is a journey, ignited by the first Psychobilly boom in Glasgow, that rolled onwards through The Klub Foot, The Night of the Long Knives, Trash, scootering, Billy's, The Big Rumbles and life on the road with bottom-rung psycho band The Rednecks.

Offering a unique perspective on the Psychobilly phenomenon, LET¹S WRECK is a punter's-eye view of the bands, venues, clothing, haircuts, lifestyle and people that are all an essential part of this most underground genre of British street music.

96 pages of Rockin' goodness, containing photographs & images from almost two decades of Psychobilly.

**VINYL DEMENTIA: The Psychobilly & Trash Record Guide Part 1. 1981-87**

Published by STORMSCREEN PRODUCTIONS
ISBN 0954624912

This 28 page A5 magazine offers full-page reviews of 20 of the most influential releases of the early 1980's, including groundbreaking slabs of infected vinyl from THE METEORS, THE SHARKS, GUANA BATZ, FRENZY, THE RICOCHETS, THE STING-RAYS, THE VIBES, DEMENTED ARE GO, UG & THE CAVEMEN, THE COFFIN NAILS, SKITZO, THE KREWMEN & KING KURT and key compilations such as "STOMPING AT THE KLUB FOOT", "ZORCH FACTOR ONE", "THESE CATS AIN'T NUTHIN BUT TRASH", "TRASH ON THE TUBE" & "HELL'S BENT ON ROCKIN". Each review features details of the original release and current availability on CD. All wrapped in a full-colour cover.

All titles available direct from

http://stores.shop.ebay.co.uk/stormscreen-productions

Also available from Raucous Records,
Amazon and all sussed bookshops.